I0526513

Murder at the College

by

P.H. Turner

Copyright Notice
This is a work of fiction. Names, characters, places, and incidents are either the product of the author's imagination or are used fictitiously, and any resemblance to actual persons living or dead, business establishments, events, or locales, is entirely coincidental.

Murder at the College

COPYRIGHT © 2023 by Patricia Headstream Turner

All rights reserved. No part of this book may be used or reproduced in any manner whatsoever without written permission of the author or The Wild Rose Press, Inc. except in the case of brief quotations embodied in critical articles or reviews.
Contact Information: info@thewildrosepress.com

Cover Art by *Tina Lynn Stout*

The Wild Rose Press, Inc.
PO Box 708
Adams Basin, NY 14410-0708
Visit us at www.thewildrosepress.com

Publishing History
First Edition, 2024
Trade Paperback ISBN 978-1-5092-5551-1
Digital ISBN 978-1-5092-5552-8

Published in the United States of America

Dedication

Once again, to my family.

Chapter 1

The ringing pierced Quinn Kane's sleep like an ice pick driving into her head. When she reached for her phone, every muscle in her entire body screamed from going three rounds with her kickboxing coach yesterday. She wished she hadn't closed the bar with the Rockin' Rollin' Derby girls last night. She'd cheered her voice raw for her best friend and then matched the Derby Girls drink for drink. Those Derby Girls could hold their liquor.

"Hello," she croaked.

"Good morning, Quinn." It was her boss, lawyer James Meadows. "Sorry to call so early, but one of our clients, Paul Loughty, a drama professor at the Denver Arts College, was murdered last night. His brother called this morning and wants to meet."

Her brain was working well enough that she remembered most murderers were family or people the deceased knew. "Was he arrested?"

"No, the police arrived at Ben's door this morning to notify him as the next of kin. He cut them off when they started to ask questions and told them he would talk when he had an attorney present. He'll be here in an hour. Can you make it?"

"Absolutely." The headache behind her eyes beat out a rhythm like a jazz percussionist. All she could think about was mainlining coffee.

"Good. One more thing," her boss said. "Deke Bystrom is the detective assigned to the case."

Great. Now, she was batting zero for two. Nursing a hangover and facing her nemesis, Detective Bystrom. It was seven thirty on a cold December Monday. Her week could only get better, couldn't it?

"When you get here, we'll discuss how you will handle Bystrom. I have news from Judge Hartley's courtroom you'll be happy to hear. See you soon."

Quinn rolled out of bed slowly, holding her head in both hands. Lousy news before coffee was the worst, and Bystrom on the case was a problem. He'd promised to make her life a living hell after they locked horns on the Nelson case over two years ago, and he had the power to do it. Worse, there were rumors that Bystrom was connected to someone with influence who kept him on the force. If Bystrom called his godfather for help, she couldn't think about that now. She would crawl back into bed and pull the covers over her head.

Quinn groaned when she bent down to put on her slippers. She headed to her dollhouse-sized kitchen, only six steps from her bedroom, but this morning, it was like climbing Long's Peak. She had two goals: to drink a pot of coffee and keep her job as the investigator for the Meadows Law Firm.

Quinn's pup, Charley, waited impatiently in the kitchen, wagging her stubby tail. She knew it was time for breakfast if Quinn was up. She was a growing girl, part standard poodle, part giant schnauzer, and covered in wavy chestnut brown curls. Six months ago, it had been love at first sight when Charley could sit in Quinn's lap. Now her paws were as big around as teacups, and she stood thigh high. If Charley got much bigger, she might have to find a larger house.

Quinn set the coffee to brew first. Then, she bent over to scoop kibble out of the thirty-pound bag and discovered the drummer in her head was now playing a new number that included cymbals.

After her third cup, Quinn was feeling human again. Charley wanted to play, but any sudden movement on her part was out of the question. She rubbed the dog's soft ears. The dog was her doppelganger with her masses of brown ringlets and brown eyes, though Quinn thought the curls looked better on Charley than on her. She'd never thought she was beautiful, but her grandmother, who had raised her, always told her that time faded beauty, but good sense and an even temperament lasted a lifetime.

She downed a granola bar and took her fourth cup of coffee to the shower, only a few steps from the kitchen. Her 1930s bungalow was a seven-hundred-square foot classic one-story brown brick with two bedrooms. One of which was so small it would barely house an elf. She'd turned it into an office with a child-size desk and a chair. She'd made the house hers by painting the walls a warm neutral and furnishing it with second-hand furniture. The mattress was the only new thing in the house. She liked to think her home was shabby chic, but it probably screamed cheap secondhand. She loved it anyway, and best of all, she lived next door to Trixie Knight, her best friend and all-star jammer for the Derby girls—when she wasn't doing secret work for a company contracted with the government. She wondered how Trixie felt this morning after Quinn drove her home from the bar and put her to bed.

Quinn showered and dressed for work but couldn't go until Charley did her business. She hated leaving the pup in the house all day but hesitated to put in a dog door. Any dog door Charley could climb through would be big enough for a burglar to squeeze through. After Charley raced inside, Quinn got her thirty-eight from the gun safe by the door and told her pup she'd return around noon.

Quinn slogged across the ice-crusted lawn toward her car, wishing the one-car garage at the back edge of the property was usable, but it leaned precariously into the wind. It would blow over into Trixie's yard if she didn't have it demolished soon. She was scraping snow off the windshield when Trixie came out her front door armed with a snow shovel and waved. An avid weightlifter, Trixie looked and acted more like a Trixie than the *Patricia* her mother tagged her with at birth.

"Good morning. How are you feeling?"

Trixie pantomimed her head blowing up. "Shh, not so loud. I could do with a full breakfast and a gallon of coffee. What do you say we go to the diner up the street?"

"I wish I could, but Meadows just called. We have a new client coming in. How about sharing a pizza tonight?"

Trixie gave her a thumbs up. "I'll be home from practice around eight."

"See you then."

Quinn drove past the mountains of dirty snow the plows left piled at the end of each block. It was the season of rivulets of filthy water leaking from the snowpack during the day and refreezing at night, leaving behind black ice. Winter would hold Denver in its grip for months.

Heavy snow fell before Quinn reached the feeder

road out of her neighborhood. She had put new tires on her car this winter, probably doubling its value. She kept it because it was paid for, and her grandmother had helped her buy it.

Frail fingers of sunlight tried to push through the clouds but lost the battle. She was rewarded with only a thin wisp of warm air when she cranked the car heater on high. A working heater was a must when she found the courage to take on a car payment. The air was so bone-breaking cold this morning that her breath fogged the windshield.

She turned the radio to the local news station. A reporter, nearly breathless with excitement, was talking about the gruesome murder of a famous playwright and gifted drama professor at the Denver Arts College. Just what Quinn didn't need. The media slavering over the story and complicating her investigation. Maybe Meadows wouldn't want to represent the murdered man's brother, and she would be free of the complications of nosy reporters.

Chapter 2

Quinn parked in the law firm's garage and walked through the heated sky bridge to Meadows' suite of offices on the top floor of the adjacent building. She brushed a few stray brown dog hairs from her black pants. She thought she looked presentable before she entered the elegant but understated reception area.

Meadows graduated from Harvard Law, so the office had more of a modern Back Bay vibe than a Queen City of the Plains look. Dark wood floors set off the cream walls, and a floor-to-ceiling glass wall looked over the Denver skyline. Leather sofas and chairs were strategically placed around dark wood tables, and geometrically shaped light fixtures filled the room with soft light.

She stopped at the desk of Meadows' paralegal. Martha was a trim, late middle-aged woman who ran his schedule and managed the office. More importantly, she knew the firm's history as well as where all the files were kept. "Mr. Meadows is in a state over Paul Loughty's murder," she said. "A colleague found the body this morning in the Green Room."

Quinn had worked as a stagehand for high school productions long enough to know the Green Room was where actors waited to go on stage. She wondered what the professor was doing alone in the theater on a Sunday evening.

"But I have some good news for you," Martha continued. "Mr. Meadows finally okayed the purchase of that facial recognition software you've been wanting. I put the order in this morning. Maybe he'll quit fussing about how much it costs."

Quinn smiled, thinking it was about time. "Thanks. Let me know when it gets here." Meadows didn't understand the caliber of technology it took to do her job well. She would make sure he got his money's worth.

She found her boss's door open and Meadows at his desk. He'd been a fullback on his college team and still carried an impressive build, even with the middle-aged spread. He was known for his colorful suspenders and matching bowties at court appearances. Today, he was decked out in fiery red suspenders and a red plaid bow tie. Any other lawyer sporting such sartorial splendor might worry the jury would write him off as a show pony, but not Meadows. He held juries in the palm of his hand.

She knocked on the door frame, and he looked up over his half-glasses and motioned her in. Quinn sat in one of the two gray leather wingback chairs facing his expansive mahogany desk.

He tapped his reading glasses on his desk. "I've known the Loughty family for decades. They were friends, as well as clients. The parents have passed, and Paul has been my client for nearly two decades. He and Ben are identical twins; I never could tell them apart until Ben got into his teens and dressed like a punk." He shook his head and leaned back in his chair. "I can't believe Paul's dead."

"How was he killed?"

"Shot twice in the head. He was found dead on the

sofa in the Green Room when the scene shop foreman came to work this morning." Meadows folded his arms across his chest. "Paul was incredibly talented, but no one's perfect, and there were problems. I'm representing him in a civil suit accusing him of sexual misconduct, and the case isn't going away now that he's dead. The plaintiff will try to collect a judgment from Paul's estate."

"Sounds like someone might have wanted him dead."

"The young woman who brought the suit is Emily Halmstad. I doubt she killed him. We've made her a generous offer to settle, and we'll pay just to clear the matter. Another student brought a suit, though I don't think it will amount to anything. I'll get the files for you to read."

"It sounds like Dr. Loughty might have had a history of inappropriate behavior with his students."

Meadows nodded. "Paul's weakness was enjoying the pleasures of the casting couch. Let's hope no one else comes forward with a complaint. I'm curious to see Ben. I haven't seen him since he moved back to Denver, and Paul didn't talk about him. The Loughty family was always a tight-lipped bunch about Ben. The twins are very different men. Paul was always a go-getter, at the top of his high school class, and went on to earn a doctorate in theater. He's written several plays and directed one of his shows off-Broadway. He's had a stellar career.

"Then, there's Ben," Meadows went on. "He was eighteen when he was arrested and found guilty of possession with intent. His father hired me to represent him, and there wasn't much I could do but call a couple of character witnesses to the stand and plead for the court's mercy. Ben was lucky to get only two years. I went with Paul the morning Ben was released, and he looked like the same cocky little son-of-a-bitch he was when he went in. It will be interesting to see what kind of man he is now."

Ben sounds like a piece of work. An ex-con with a murky past, without two nickels to rub together. Meadows was all about making money, and Ben didn't sound like he could pay his bill. "Any qualms about taking him on as a client?"

"Let's see what he has to say for himself and if he can pay the bills."

And there it was, Meadows' top criterion for taking a client. "Does Ben inherit from Paul?"

"If that's why Ben's coming in, he'll be disappointed. Everything goes to Paul's kid, Jason. He's living in California with his mom and stepfather and is in college. I spoke to him this morning, and Jason didn't mention the will. There's time for that later when the shock has worn off, but I don't think Jason has it in him to kill his dad. He acts like an entitled little twat, tethered to his electronics. But then again, I feel the same way about my grandson."

Martha stuck her head in the door. "Morning, sir. Mr. Loughty is here to see you."

Meadows asked her to bring him back.

Ben Loughty walked in, looking like he'd just stepped off a fashion shoot in a calf-length camel hair coat over black wool slacks and an impeccably tailored white shirt. He had piercing gray eyes under dark brows and a head of thick dark hair cut fashionably long on top and short on the sides.

Ben was walking, talking eye candy for any woman starved for male companionship. Like Quinn, who'd been in a man drought for longer than she liked to remember. But, she reminded herself, he was a client and off-limits.

Though there was no penalty for looking. Unless she got caught drooling.

"Good morning, Mr. Meadows. Thank you for fitting me into your schedule." Ben shook Meadows' hand.

Ben's eyes widened with interest as he turned to Quinn.

She offered her hand. "I'm Quinn Kane, the firm's investigator."

"Ms. Kane, it's a pleasure to meet you." He took her hand, and a connection arced between them. She could tell by his eyes that Ben felt it, too.

Quinn withdrew her hand and glanced at Meadows. He was looking at the notes he'd taken and didn't see her reaction to meeting Ben. The three of them settled into their chairs.

"We're sorry to hear of Paul's death. How can we be of help?" Meadows asked.

"I need a good lawyer. Detective Bystrom came by this morning and said I should come along nicely like a good boy and answer his questions at the station. I don't want to find myself in a situation where he tries to rig up a case against me because I'm a family member and an ex-con. That's why I called you, Mr. Meadows. I want you to represent me."

Ben had a beautiful baritone voice and long-fingered, elegant hands. Quinn caught herself wondering what it would feel like to have those hands on her body.

It was an effort, but she wrestled her attention back on her boss.

Meadows handed Ben a form. "You made a wise decision to get in touch with me. Here's our client contract. Take your time, and I'll answer any questions you have."

Ben flipped through the form, gave it a perfunctory read, and scribbled his name on the bottom. He pushed it across the desk to Meadows.

"Thank you," Meadows said, taking the document. "As my client, you have an attorney-client privilege. Anything you tell me is confidential, and no one can force you to reveal the content of our discussions. However, you lose the privilege if you discuss your case with anyone outside the firm."

"I understand," Ben said.

"Good." Meadows leaned forward in his chair. "Let's get a little background out of the way. When did you last see Paul?"

"We had lunch together last Friday and talked on the phone Sunday. We made plans to have a late dinner and watch the Broncos game at his house after he finished the rehearsal on Sunday evening. He called me back in a couple of hours and said he couldn't make it."

"Did he say why?" Meadows asked.

Ben sat back and folded his arms over his chest. "He told me he was going to meet his girlfriend, Margarite Mancini, and break up with her. She was a student of his."

"Were you surprised that he wanted to break up with her?" Suddenly, a door slammed, and heavy footsteps and angry voices passed outside Meadows' office. "Sorry about that," he said pleasantly as they faded away. "We're handling a contentious divorce."

Ben had been staring at the floor. When he looked up, Quinn saw the pain and loss in his face. "Paul was unhappy. He was a free spirit. He needed time alone to create and recharge, and he couldn't get it through Margarite's thick head. She was so emotional and needy that she was draining the life out of Paul, and it was tearing him apart. He met her in the theater because it was private. If she went nuts on him, he wouldn't be embarrassed in front of people."

"Did she have a habit of embarrassing him? Meadows asked.

"Three months ago, I was at a dinner party at his house. Paul was running late, which wasn't unusual for him, but Margarite was angry. She went upstairs, cut up all his dress pants, and threw the scraps out the bedroom window onto the front lawn. Paul hated that kind of crap. And lately, Margarite had been bugging him to marry her. My brother was never going to marry her—or anyone."

"It sounds like you didn't like Margarite," Quinn said.

Ben turned toward her. "I don't like her, and Paul knew how I felt."

"Was that a problem between you and your brother?" Quinn asked, looking into the depths of his beautiful gray eyes.

"No, we were always honest with each other."

"Do you think Margarite killed him?" Meadows asked.

"She could have. She has a terrible temper and not much impulse control. She'd convinced herself that Paul was going to marry her. When he told her he was breaking it off and there wasn't going to be a wedding, she could have killed him."

"Have you spoken to her since Paul died?" Meadows asked.

Ben shook his head.

"Good. I suggest you have no contact with Ms. Mancini. Don't tell anyone else that Paul told you he would stay alone in the theater after rehearsal."

"Right. If Detective Bystrom found out I knew Paul would be there alone, he'd arrest me. I guess you want to know where I was last night. I was home, watching the evening news, then the Broncos game, by myself."

"Can anyone confirm that?"

"Unfortunately, no."

"Quinn will go around and check with your neighbors and see if one of them heard or saw you," Meadows said. "Where do you live?"

There was a soft tap on Meadows' door. Looking contrite, Martha stuck her head in and said a young associate needed a word.

"It will have to wait," Meadows told her.

"I'm sorry for the interruption," Meadows told Ben.

"It's no problem. I'm renting a condo in the Jefferson Building in the Cherry Creek area."

Meadows made a note of the address. "Did your brother have enemies?"

Ben frowned. "I wouldn't call them enemies. He had the usual conflicts with colleagues. It's a small department. Dr. Henry Beckett is the head of the Drama Department. He favored my brother because Paul raised money from donors. The other faculty were jealous, but Paul never seemed worried about it. He had Dr. Beckett in his pocket, and that's all that mattered."

"Who were your brother's friends?" Quinn asked.

"I don't know that he had any friends. Paul was a workaholic. He was busy all the time, directing or writing a play, raising money, or traveling all over the country to recruit high school students for the program. He stayed with me in Baltimore a couple of times when he was recruiting. His job was his life, except for Jason and me."

"Have you talked with Jason or his mother this morning?" Meadows asked.

Ben nodded. "I called him after the police talked to me. The L.A.P.D. had already been by to see him. He'll be here in the morning. I haven't spoken to Paul's ex-wife in years."

"I look forward to seeing Jason again," Meadows said. "I have a few more questions." He tapped his pen on the edge of his desk. "Is there anything relevant to Paul's death I need to know about you?"

Ben frowned. "The curse that never goes away. A misspent youth as the black sheep of the family. I've been clean for over two decades and have had no problems with the police."

"Excellent. We don't want any complications. Where were you employed before you returned to Denver?"

Ben relaxed and seemed happy to talk about his work. "I worked as an independent diamond merchant, and it was a good life. I traveled the world, hunting the perfect stones for my clients. But when I neared the dreaded forty, I realized how important family is. I wanted to spend time with Paul and put down roots."

"You're retired?" Meadows asked.

Ben smiled and shook his head. "No, I bought the

old Queen City Hotel on Colfax Avenue and opened the Starlight Lounge. I'll carve out two apartments on the second floor and live on the third. I got hooked on saving historical buildings when I spent a summer in a thatched village called Minster Lovell in the Cotswolds. The council wanted to level a lovely little cottage from the fifteenth century. I couldn't stand by and let that happen, so I bought it." He laughed. "I had no idea what I was getting it to, but I loved the restoration work. I already have another project in mind."

"Oh?" Quinn asked, mainly because she liked the cadence of his voice and the deep timbre. Anything to keep him talking. "Here in Denver?"

He nodded and seemed eager to talk of work. "The Bluebird Theater, down the street from the Starlight. But I'll have to get a grant from the Denver Historic Preservation Fund before starting the restoration. My hobby is expensive."

Quinn thought Ben must have done very well as a diamond buyer. Property on Colfax wasn't cheap, nor was restoration work or a rental in the Cherry Creek area.

Meadows brought the conversation back to the murder. "Paul was a high-profile person. There will be a significant amount of media interest in the case. His agent has already called me and asked that we guard his reputation. I suggest you don't talk to the press. Don't even say *no comment* because they'll twist that around until it sounds like you're guilty of something. And don't discuss your brother's death with anyone unless I'm there to advise you. We represent you now, and you have the firm's full resources."

"Will do. My history with the police is not pleasant."

"Do you have any questions for me?"

"No, I trust you to take care of things, but there is one thing. I want to be a part of the team."

"If you're charged with a crime, your best bet is to let me and my staff handle your case," Meadows said.

Ben shook his head. "With all due respect to your reputation for being a shark in the courtroom, it's my ass in the wringer. I won't stand on the sidelines. Is this going to be a deal-breaker for you?"

"You just hired the best defense attorney in the city," Meadows promised. "We'll make it happen."

"Fair enough." Ben stood and slipped his arms into a beautiful tailor-made overcoat. He looked at Quinn and said, "I hope my working with you won't be a problem, Ms. Kane. It was nice to meet you."

Quinn watched him walk to the doorway with Meadows. The man had class. He was gorgeous, and every move was polished and elegant, but she didn't want to work with him.

Chapter 3

James Meadows closed the door behind Ben and lost no time giving Quinn orders. "Do your usual job of rock turning and information gathering. We have to be prepared if Ben's arrested for murder. Like always, I'd rather not know how you find what you dig up."

"Right," she answered. James Meadows had a law license to protect and wanted plausible deniability of what she did. He would throw her under the bus to protect his license if she was caught snooping in the wrong place. She hadn't been caught yet and wasn't planning to go down in a blaze of shame this time. "Do you think he killed his brother?"

"I don't see any reason to believe he did, but I didn't think anyone would shoot Paul either," Meadows said. "When I see a client in my office, I only see a tiny fraction of who they are, and what I see is a tightly curated persona the client wants to show me. Once, I had a client who came in to make a will. I thought he was an ordinary guy until three years later when he was arrested for four gruesome murders in southwestern Colorado. I went home and told my wife, 'If Larry Don Yacker is a serial killer, there's no one we can trust." He shrugged. "Ben could have killed his brother."

"What do you think about what he said about Margarite?" Quinn asked.

Meadows lowered himself into his chair. "We don't

have confirmation she was with Paul Sunday night or that she's unstable. Ben might be blowing smoke up my pant leg to divert attention from himself."

Blunt but true. "I'll track down Margarite today and talk to her."

"Good, let me know what she has to say for herself. Now that Ben's a client, I'll call the campus police and request a copy of any surveillance footage of the Alderberry Theater from Sunday night."

"Thank you. I'll need that as soon as possible."

As Meadows leaned back, his chair groaned in protest. "I had an interesting conversation yesterday with Amos Daniels. He's the attorney who brought suit on behalf of a client against the Denver P.D. for violating his client's civil rights. Bystrom is a named co-defendant in that suit."

Quinn knew her least favorite detective was named in a court case before Judge Hartley but didn't know the details. Only another lawyer like Meadows would.

"Amos convinced Judge Hartley that Bystrom was keeping a secret evidence file against his client. The Judge demanded the police make all their files on the accused available to the defense team following the Brady doctrine. Amos and his team spend days in the basement of the old police headquarters going through files. That's where Bystrom kept the secret file, and no one was allowed access to the basement unless they worked for him. Amos said the amount of evidence he found in the hidden files was staggering, and much of it was worthy of an A-list crime novel. The case will be tied up in court for weeks, and I'm sure the Denver P.D. will appeal if the Judge rules against them, which means there won't be a decision to help us if Ben's arrested.

You'll have to watch yourself. Bystrom is under the gun, and Paul's murder is high-profile. Bystrom needs to look like a good cop, and he won't have any qualms about how he makes that happen. Making a quick arrest of Ben and closing the Loughty case will make him look like solid gold. If I have to defend Ben on a murder charge, I don't want to be blindsided by a secret file."

"I'll do my best," Quinn promised.

"It might be harder than you think. The rumor is that Bystrom has a godfather, and I think it's true. Bystrom's slicker than goose shit, and he hasn't lasted this long on the force without someone running interference for him. Every time Bystrom is hauled before Internal Affairs, he comes out smelling like a rose. He's doing something for the godfather in return for the protection he's getting. Find out who this asshole's godfather is and what Bystrom's doing for him."

Great, three jobs. "Consider it done," she said. All she had to do was find out who the godfather was, what Bystrom did for him, and prove the client innocent.

Meadows stood and shrugged on his jacket, indicating the meeting was over. "You're going to have to work with Ben. Structure it how you want, and don't let him compromise your investigation. Just make it happen. I'm going to the courthouse and see what the morning gossip is."

Though Quinn's hangover was better, the drummer was still practicing his snare drum solo. She didn't see how she could possibly work with Ben. People wouldn't open up and talk freely about Paul Loughty with the dead man's brother hanging off her shoulder, but she owed James Meadows. She had been green as grass when he took a chance and hired her, and she was still proving herself. If she did well and built her reputation, she would have a shot at opening her own business, Kane Investigations.

Aim high was her motto, and she better not fail now.

****

Quinn's first move was to go to Ben's condominium complex in Cherry Hill and talk to his neighbors. No one had heard a peep from his apartment Sunday night, and no one saw him in the public areas. She called Ben, but it went straight to voice mail. She left a message and asked him to call Meadows' office and give his consent for his cell phone records to be released to the firm.

Quinn knew she needed the talents of Truck Tucker, her hacker extraordinaire who knew his way around the Dark Web, had spies in police stations, and had his finger on the pulse of everyone in Denver's business community. She didn't discuss anything with Truck over the phone—or leave a paper trail—because she turned to him for all those things that might cost her license if she were caught. Their business was in person only.

Truck had earned his nickname while he was inside for a couple of years and passed the time lifting weights and studying computer science on the state's dollar. After he was released, he looked like a jacked-up two-ton truck. He had put his newly learned computer skills to work with the infamous Blackhawk Hacker Group until he quit and started his own business. If what she paid him was indicative of what he made, he earned good money.

She headed east toward Kwon's Bar in Korea Town and passed by her alma mater, Front Range State University. She had enjoyed her five years on campus while she earned a journalism degree. Her grandmother had cheered her on as she shuttled from class to work and back. After she graduated, she worked for a small weekly paper covering the Roaring Fork Valley. A steady diet of cheap packets of Asian noodles and a long drive to Denver to see her grandmother convinced Quinn she wasn't cut out to be a journalist. She took her curiosity and investigative skills to the law firm. She liked her job and needed to keep it. Those student loans were a bear to pay off.

She pulled up in front of Kwon's bar, a squat two-story, drab brown building in Korea Town, which probably hadn't changed much since the first Kwon barkeep cooked booze in the alley during Prohibition. Truck lived above the bar; she didn't know—because she'd never asked—the exact nature of his relationship with the Kwon family other than as their tenant. The Kwons were associated with Kkangpae, a South Korean criminal group that laundered money through Korean-owned small businesses, including the bar. The gang demanded loyalty and cash from the business owners, who promptly paid. While the exact size of the Korean mob in Denver was hard to gauge, the Kkangpae was large enough to keep a stranglehold on the neighborhood.

Quinn pushed through the carved front door into the bar. The decor was left over from the Jazz Era. The dark wood floors were so warped it was like walking on a ship's deck plowing through an angry sea, but the bar had a warm, friendly vibe and served as the favorite neighborhood watering hole. By the front windows, wizened old men played Baduk, a game of strategy where opponents battled to capture their competitor's stones. If tourists stumbled in off the street for a drink, they'd never guess that the Kwons were part of a criminal gang.

Quinn waved at Mi Cha, the daughter of the current proprietor, who was working behind the bar. She went to a booth tucked in the back where Truck held office.

He was drinking coffee, probably spiked with his favorite blended whiskey. He looked up and smiled. "Babe, get yourself a coffee."

She declined the offer with a shake of her head and slid into the booth across from him. "I need information on our new client, Ben Loughty. His brother was murdered last night at the Denver Arts College. I want a Dark Web search and to know what your spies at the D.P.D. are saying about Loughty's murder."

"You know I don't have spies. Such a highly connotative word."

"Okay then. What do your *intelligence officers* know about the Loughty murder?"

Truck grinned. "I'll find out."

"Good. One more thing. I need to know the name of the guy who is powerful enough to keep Detective Bystrom on the job."

Truck waited to answer until the uproarious laughter from the Baduk players and the rattle of the stones tossed on the table died down. "Bystrom's a nasty piece of work."

"That he is, but he's the detective on the case. You'll ask for the usual consultant rate for the Meadows firm?"

Truck nodded and took another sip of coffee. "What are you looking for on the Dark Web?"

Quinn shrugged. "Whatever it is that's making me uneasy about Ben."

Truck nodded. "Give me a couple of days."

****

While Quinn drove away from Kwon's, she used her cell phone to call an investigator in Los Angeles. He was a one-man shop who worked for a well-vetted list of clients, and she was happy to be on his list. She caught him in his office, and after a brief greeting and catch-up, she got down to business and hired him to check the whereabouts of Paul Loughty's son, Jason, and his ex-wife, on the night Paul was murdered. He promised to put a rush on it.

Her next stop was Margarite Mancini's apartment. She was curious about what Paul's college-age girlfriend would be like.

Margarite's apartment was in a rundown building near the Denver Arts College that looked like it needed a good scrubbing or a fresh coat of paint. As Quinn climbed the outside stairs to the girl's second-floor apartment, a frigid December wind whipped up the stairwell. Quinn passed two units with grimy windows overlooking the parking lot below. When Quinn rapped on Margarite's door, the curtains in the adjacent apartment parted, and a young man with a straggly soul patch looked out. When he caught Quinn looking at him, he disappeared behind the curtain.

She knocked again, and a young woman with long, dark hair and legs as slender as a colt's opened the door. "Who are you?"

Quinn held up her business card. "Quinn Kane. I work for the Meadows Law Firm. We represent Paul Loughty. I'm looking for Margarite Mancini."

She gushed, "Oh, you're one of Paul's lawyers. I'm Margarite." She stepped back and opened the door to let Quinn inside.

Margarite caught Quinn looking around the cramped apartment and said, "Sorry, it's a dump even if it was clean."

The front room had two upholstered chairs that had seen better days and a table that didn't look sturdy enough to hold the large flat-screen television balanced tenuously on it. The place was small enough for Quinn to take in the kitchen nook off to one side, and down a short hallway was a bedroom with a rumpled bed. "I know this is a difficult time for you, but I have to ask you a few questions."

"Have a seat," Margarite said.

Quinn took one of the chairs, but Margarite paced the room as though she was too wired to be still. She had large dark eyes, beautiful olive skin, and a generous mouth. The girl was stunning, even with the streaks of eye makeup smudged under her eyes and unkempt hair. It was easy to see why Paul was attracted. "Just to clear up any misconception," Quinn said, "I'm the firm's private investigator."

Margarite turned at the window to face Quinn. "Did Paul tell you about me? That we were getting married?"

"I never had the privilege of meeting Dr. Loughty, but Ben told me you and Paul were close."

Stopping in her tracks, Margarite brought her hands to her hips. "Ben's a lying sack of shit. Paul and I weren't just close. We were getting married."

No love lost between Ben and Margarite.

Quinn was about to ask the girl about her beef with Ben when Margarite threw her arms wide and wailed, "How could anyone hurt Paul? Everyone loved him." She snatched a tissue from the box on the table and dabbed her eyes. "I loved him so much." One fist came

24

to her mouth as she sobbed. "I can't believe I'll never see him again, and he'll never know our baby."

Ben hadn't mentioned a baby. Quinn wondered if he even knew about the pregnancy. "When are you due?"

Margarite grabbed a tissue and wiped her nose. She sat in the chair next to Quinn's and sighed. "Late July. We just found out."

"Congratulations. New life is always a reason to celebrate. Do you have someone to help you?"

"My mom. We haven't always gotten along, but she's happy about my baby." She cupped her belly. "I'll always have a part of Paul."

"Yes, and it's good you have your mother to help. When did you last see Paul?"

"Sunday. I took sushi to his office for lunch."

"Did he often work on the weekends?"

She shrugged. "Paul was always working. He knew I was mad at him for not spending more time with me, so he promised to take me to Idaho Springs next weekend to make it up to me. It was going to be so special. Just the two of us. Now, I'll never get to do that with him."

Somehow, Margarite always flipped the conversation back to her relationship with Paul, the man she claimed would marry her. Was she prone to flights of fantasy? "Again, I'm sorry to ask personal questions, but did Paul seem upset or frightened when you saw him on Sunday?"

Margarite shook her hair back from her face. "Everything was fine. Paul was happy. He was working on some last-minute changes to the technical script for his new play. He had a rehearsal with the tech crew Sunday night." She broke down and launched into another crying jag. "I couldn't stay long at lunch. I had a test I had to study for, and now, I'll never see him again."

Quinn gave her a moment before asking, "Was Paul having difficulties with anyone?"

A sly look came over Margarite's face. "Maybe, Roxie Ryland. She's his student assistant this term. Paul dumped her for me, but Roxie couldn't take her eyes off him. You know what I mean. Every time I looked at her, she was watching Paul."

To Quinn, it sounded like it was more of a problem for Margarite than for Paul. "Did that bother you?"

Again, she shook back her long hair. "Of course not. Paul wasn't interested in Roxie."

"What about with his colleagues? Any problems there?"

"He never talked to me about that stuff. When we were alone, we were in our little world."

"Did Paul and his brother get along?"

"Ben is a walking clusterfuck. Did you know he went to prison? He can't hold a job. He mooched off Paul. My man is the good twin. Good twin, bad twin, get it?"

"Do you mean Paul supported Ben financially?"

"Paul put up the money for the Starlight Lounge and covered Ben's monthly bills. Ben could never have built that bar and run it."

"It sounds like you don't like Ben."

"I hate him. I told Paul he needed to cut his ties to Ben, but he was too softhearted to do it." She looked at Quinn earnestly. "Ben killed my sweet man."

"How do you think that happened?"

"Simple. Ben met him after rehearsal and demanded more money. Paul wouldn't give it to him, so Ben killed him."

Nothing Margarite said fit with Ben's story. "Did Paul mention he was meeting someone after rehearsal?"

Suddenly, the girl looked wary. "No."

"Where were you on Sunday night?"

"Here. I told you that I had to study."

"Can anyone vouch for your whereabouts Sunday night?"

Margarite shook her head.

"Are you sure you didn't see Paul? Maybe talk on the phone with him after lunch?"

"No, I told you I didn't see him after I left his office. You're trying to confuse me." Margarite launched to her feet, clenching and unclenching her fists. "You're like the cops, trying to trick me into saying stuff that's not true. You work for Paul's lawyer. You're supposed to be helping me."

"The firm represents Paul's estate," Quinn said. "If you need a lawyer, I can give you the names of several good ones."

"I don't need a lawyer." She ran to the door and threw it open. "Get out. You're making me crazy, and it's not good for my baby."

Quinn wrapped her coat around her and picked her way around the ice forming on the stairs. Margarite could be an imaginative liar who was playing the part of a woman whose lover was murdered and left to raise their child alone.

On the other hand, Ben had spun a compelling story about his work as a diamond merchant and his love of restoring old buildings. It was hard for Quinn to believe he was lying, but she might have her head turned by his looks and charm. It would be easy enough to find out if Margarite was telling the truth about Ben's finances.

Chapter 4

When Quinn returned to the law office, she found two thick files on her desk. A note from Meadows explained they were the case files on the civil suits against Paul Loughty.

Quinn skimmed Emily Halmstad's suit which Meadows had said the firm would settle out of court. The lawsuit accused Paul of taking advantage of his position as Director of Theater by sexually abusing Emily, and then persuading her to keep quiet about what happened between them. Emily claimed that Paul had forced her to have sex with him in the Green Room after an evening rehearsal. In return for her silence, she claimed Paul promised to place her with the Windy City Thespians, a professional group of actors in Chicago.

There were no eyewitnesses to the assault, and eighteen-year-old Emily didn't report the incident to the police. Because she waited a year to make a complaint, there was no physical or biological evidence, so the case hinged on witness statements. Quinn flipped through the file to the depositions from cast members. A male cast member who had seen Emily remain with Paul that night testified, *What did she think Paul wanted with her? Intellectual conversation at eleven at night? Emily put out for everyone. She just wants the cash.*

Other male cast members made similar statements about Emily. However, the women were sympathetic to her. Several indicated Paul had offered them special favors in return for sex. No wonder Meadows wanted to settle. The Halmstead file left Quinn wondering if Paul's murder was related to how he treated female students.

She made a few notes before picking up the second file. A message was attached to the front. Tiberius Clark-Watson had withdrawn his case that morning. Quinn wondered if his parents were sci-fi movie fans or had named their son after Rome's second emperor. She opened the file.

Tiberius had claimed Dr. Loughty's overt favoritism to women violated his rights under Title IX and the U.S. Constitution. The case sounded unique, like an argument a lawyer would love to bring before a judge. Yet Tiberius had withdrawn the case.

Quinn noted the student's phone number and wondered why Meadows thought it was important that she read the two suits, particularly since Tiberius had dropped his. She hadn't shared with Meadows what Margarite had told her about the affair between Roxie Ryland and Paul Loughty.

One student's complaint of being a victim of coerced sex might be overlooked. What if she was seeing the tip of an iceberg? A sex for favors scandal involving a murdered professor was a scandal the college would want to keep quiet. No parent wanted to send their kid to a school where the professors preyed on the students.

It would be interesting to talk to Paul's colleagues. What if they were involved? Quinn felt a nasty jolt when she thought of Ben. Had he indulged himself in his brother's appetites?

She set the files aside, typed the Loughty surname into a search engine, and discovered it was an ancient British name. Fewer than fifty individuals in the United States carried the name. It should be easy to find Ben's story. However, after logging into her usual go-to databases, she was surprised to see Ben's digital breadcrumb trail was sparse. She found the deed to the Queen City Hotel and the title to a classic 1972 powder-white coupe. She smiled when she saw the handful of speeding tickets. All the fines had been paid, but the nearly fifty-year-old classic must run fast enough to annoy the cops. The local paper offered several articles about Ben's preservation work in Denver and his work in the Cotswolds. The digital trail ended there. There were no social media accounts.

Satisfied the news stories verified Ben's explanation of his current work, Quinn continued her search. Though Truck was better on the Dark Web than her, she could find her way around. Meadows was always pleased with the depth of her research, but he would have had a stroke if he knew she bought cryptocurrency to pay for information on the Dark Web. He might fire her if he ever discovered she buried the costs in her expense report.

Quinn turned on her virtual private network, shielding her searches from curious hackers, and used an encrypted browser to safeguard her anonymity while surfing the Dark Web. She couldn't be too careful, considering what was for sale on the Dark Web: women, kids, dope, guns, and the services of a hitman. Much of the information that many people considered private, such as credit card and bank account numbers and their social security numbers, was for sale. Quinn used cryptocurrency to purchase Ben's personal and business account numbers. She often paid Truck the same way, leaving no way to track the transactions to her. Meadows was greedy to read what she found, but he didn't want to know how she acquired it.

Quinn scrolled through Ben's bank account. He cleared nearly twenty thousand dollars monthly after paying the bar's expenses. The only interesting item paid from his checking account was a sizeable monthly donation to Our Lady of Sorrows Catholic Church in Baltimore. Like clockwork, the money moved electronically from his account to theirs on the first of each month. There were plenty of Catholic churches in Denver, yet he donated to a church thousands of miles away. There was a story wrapped inside those donations, and she wanted to know it.

Quinn couldn't find any other bank accounts in Ben's name. He had to have another account to build out the top two floors of the Starlight and purchase and renovate the Bluebird Theater. Ben must have money stashed offshore, which wasn't illegal. She'd read plenty of reports from finance experts who believe almost half the world's capital flows through offshore banks. Even senators parked cash out of the country while the little guy worked on his taxes, trying to figure out how much money he must fork over.

It was surprisingly easy for Quinn to buy the number of an account registered in the Caymans in the name of Ben Loughty, LLC, a private corporation of one. He must have been a *very* successful diamond merchant. Finding the numbered account was as far as her hacking skills could take her. Truck would have to find out how wealthy Ben was.

She closed the browser and wondered if Paul knew about Ben's offshore account. Maybe Paul became suspicious and asked hard questions, and Ben killed him, though that didn't fit her first impressions of Ben. She corrected herself. She didn't know enough about Ben to draw any conclusions. He could be like Larry Don Yacker, the serial killer who fooled Meadows into believing he was a regular guy.

It bothered her that Ben had so little information online. She wondered if he had his personal information professionally wiped or, perhaps, he was a technophobe, but she didn't believe he was. She thought he must have hired a cleaner to erase his online past. If he did, what was he hiding?

It was well past six when she gathered her things to leave the office. The staff had already packed up and locked their office doors. Quinn closed her office, still chafed she had to work with Ben. She decided to surprise him at the Starlight Lounge and lay some ground rules.

She was driving out of the parking garage when her phone rang. Meadows didn't usually call this late in the day. "Quinn, I've just heard from a friend who sits on your State Licensure Board. Detective Bystrom filed a complaint against you, claiming you misrepresented yourself to Margarite Mancini by telling her you were a police officer."

"I would never cross that line. I didn't misrepresent myself."

"Did you record it?"

She sucked in a breath. She hadn't. A careless moment like this could jeopardize her license and her livelihood. She could lose everything she'd worked for. Meadows demanded perfection from everyone who worked for him. She'd made a bad mistake. "I didn't record it, but I didn't see evidence that Margarite recorded it either."

"I suppose we will know soon enough if she did.

You know better than this, Quinn. You gave Bystrom an opportunity to make trouble, and he grabbed it and ran with it. The integrity of my firm is at stake. Get an attorney and take care of this."

"I'll take care of it. Thank you for letting me know the complaint was filed."

She hung up, thinking Bystrom was taking a risk going after her with a false complaint when he was involved in a lawsuit. Meadows was right about him. Bystrom would do anything to close the Loughty case as quickly as possible and burnish his image of a law-and-order guy. He wanted to get her off the case and make Meadows scramble to hire another investigator. It wasn't going to happen if she could help it.

Chapter 5

Quinn was nervous as she drove to the Starlight bar. She was attracted to Ben, and he was forbidden fruit. Why did these things happen to her? She was either attracted to a man who didn't know she existed, or he was unavailable. Nothing about men had ever come easy to her. She had to stop thinking about Ben. She didn't need the complications of daydreaming about him while trying to find evidence proving his innocence. She needed to wrestle her feelings into a box and nail it shut before she saw him again.

The Starlight sat on Colfax Street in the middle of the block, between two decrepit buildings, desperate for an angel investor to rescue them. More than a hundred years ago, the gold miners had dubbed Colfax the Golden Road because it was lined with shops and stores where they bought their supplies before heading west into the mountains to prospect. When the gold played out, the street had become a red-light district. Now, businessmen like Ben were stepping in to save the historical buildings.

A slick neon script spelled out the bar's name and cast moody blue shadows over the sidewalk. The front door was carved oak with glass inserts and looked old enough to be original to the hotel. She heard jazz music and a noisy crowd when she opened the door.

The bar was packed, and Quinn elbowed her way to

the ornate wood bar that ran the building's length. Above the bar was an expanse of mirrors that reflected the exposed brick wall behind her. Antique light fixtures hung from the tin ceiling, throwing pools of soft light over the patrons.

A hip-looking mixologist plied his trade with theatrical flair. He worked on a platform, raised off the floor, giving the audience a theater-in-the-round view of his performance. A jazz group onstage in the back corner played a Coltrane tune. Quinn caught the eye of the barkeep and ordered a vodka martini.

Her drink came with the perfect amount of vermouth and a twist of lemon. She watched a sociable group of patrons push together two tables to make room for all. Other couples gravitated to the corners where high-backed leather booths gave them more privacy.

Ben circled through his customers and stopped to chat and shake hands. He moved with an athlete's grace and seemed to enjoy the company of his customers. He glanced up and smiled at her as though he sensed her watching him. "Welcome to the Starlight," he said, sitting on the bar stool beside her. "To what do I owe the pleasure?"

"Mostly business, but I'm enjoying the music."

"Are you a jazz aficionado?"

Quinn watched his eyes flash with interest. "I just know what I like. I've never seen a bar on a platform before. Was it your idea?"

"I thought it smacked of Vegas until my architect showed me pictures of bars in Harlem and Los Angeles during the roaring '20s. He sold me on the idea of going with the retro look."

"I like it. It's elegant and warm and friendly."

"Thanks. It was a labor of love. The hotel dates back to 1859 and was the first in the city to have running water and electricity. She was the city's Queen until the mines played and the guests quit coming. It was in terrible shape when I bought it, but I was able to save the original brick walls and tin ceilings." He tapped the bar with his fingers. "This isn't original. It came out of a bar on Bourbon Street in New Orleans. The original bar was most likely stolen." He smiled self-consciously. "Sorry. Paul said the hotel was all I talked about ever since I got the history bug."

"You didn't bore me." Quinn smelled oranges and turned around to see the mixologist dropping orange peels into a pot of simmering water.

"He's prepping Paul's favorite flaming cocktail, a mix of 151-proof rum and orange-flavored simple syrup. Paul loved the drama of setting a drink on fire. It will be our signature cocktail in his honor."

"How are you doing?" she asked.

"I'm at work because I didn't want to spend the evening alone."

"I'm sorry."

"Thank you." He twisted on the bar stool until his knees almost touched hers. "I think you came to talk to me about business. Let's go back to my office; it's quieter there."

They walked through a narrow hallway, past restrooms, and a roped-off staircase to his office near the exit to the alley. He stood aside for Quinn to go in first. She turned sideways in the cramped space to get past an old oak rolltop desk that nearly filled the room. She sat on a metal folding chair in front of the desk.

Ben sat beside her. "Sorry about the chairs. I don't

hold many meetings here. I prefer to meet with the staff out on the floor." The music in the bar reached a crescendo. "Sorry about the noise. It's not soundproof back here."

"It's fine." Quinn motioned to the enormous old desk. "My granddad had a rolltop desk like that when he worked in the old ordnance plant."

"So, you're a local, too."

"Yes, I've lived here all my life."

"I found the desk in this office. There was a box of old hotel records in the bottom drawer, and I gave them to the historical association. I hope the guy who worked here a century ago would like what I've done with the place."

"You've done a great job of keeping the old and mixing in the new." Quinn glanced at the pictures on the wall behind his desk. Two identical young men self-consciously stood beside girls in poufy dresses.

Ben saw her looking. "That's our senior prom night, the first time either of us wore a tux. I can't remember either girl's name."

"You look happy."

"We were. Paul and I were always close. I feel like I've lost my other half." Ben's face softened when he talked about his brother. "Part of me wants to run away to my favorite place to fish, an island off the coast of Brazil, so far off the beaten path that the tourists haven't spoiled it. Warm seas, rum shacks, and good fishing. I could while away the time there, but I can't. I have my nephew to think of."

It wasn't what Quinn expected. She hadn't pegged him as a man who would readily open up and share his feelings. Ben seemed even more attractive.

"Do you think I killed Paul?"

"I don't know who killed him."

"That wasn't what I wanted to hear, but I believe you'll find who did."

Quinn nodded. "I will. You seemed worried about Detective Bystrom this morning." She wondered if he had knowledge of Bystrom's shady past or if he was just a good judge of character. Or maybe, he knew about the Nelson case that she and Bystrom had butted heads over.

"I'm an easy mark for him. You know as well as I do that policing is a numbers game. It's not about the quality of work. It's about how many cases the cops clear. I've heard stories that would curl your hair of cops forcing a confession, framing a man, or buying a witness. Sure, some were cons, and nobody cons like a con, but there is more than a grain of truth in those stories."

Quick shook her head. "Let's not borrow trouble," she cautioned. "You haven't been charged, and you have the finest defense attorney in town on your side. I'm not shabby either."

Ben smiled. "Certainly not shabby." He leaned over in his chair and cleared his throat. "Let's talk about the eight-hundred-pound gorilla in the room. Meadows is pressuring you to work with me, and you probably don't like it." He raised one hand palm out to ward off her butting in. "I'm not a sit-around guy, but I won't be a problem for you. My future is at stake, and I have to be hands-on."

James Meadows hadn't given Quinn a choice. "We'll make it work." Maybe working with Ben wouldn't be as bad as she thought, but she still needed to lay some ground rules. "I'll need to conduct some interviews without you. People won't talk freely with the victim's brother standing by me."

"Fair enough."

There was a knock on the door, and a man opened it and stuck his head in. "Sorry, Boss. I didn't realize you had company."

"That's fine, Emilio. This is my friend, Quinn Kane." He turned to Quinn. "This is Emilio Garza, my right-hand man."

"Nice to meet you, Emilio."

Emilio nodded and smiled at Quinn.

"How can I help?" Ben asked.

"Just wanted to talk to you about one of the waitstaff."

"More trouble with Irene?" Ben asked.

"Yes, more of the same."

"I'm sorry to hear that. Draw her pay and severance from the till and walk her out."

Emilio gave a two-finger salute in Ben's direction and closed the door. "Thanks, boss. Nice to meet you, miss."

"Owning a bar isn't all glamorous," Ben said. "Sometimes you hire someone who looks perfect for the job, and it doesn't work out."

Quinn nodded her agreement. It was time to tell him about her visit with Margarite and see his reaction. "I talked to Margarite today."

"Margarite's a good actress," Ben said. "I hope she didn't fool you."

"She claims she is pregnant with Paul's child."

He shook his head. "It's not Paul's. He had a vasectomy. He told me she was pushing him to marry her because she was pregnant, and we laughed about it. Except it doesn't seem so funny now. What if Paul called her out on the lie Sunday night, and she killed him?"

"Margarite claims she was home alone Sunday night. Meadows has requested the Sunday evening surveillance footage from the college police. We'll know who was there."

The bar's back door slammed shut hard enough to reverberate in the small office. "That would be Irene leaving," Ben said. He ran his hand through his hair, mussing the thick curls. "I wish it hadn't taken Paul so long to agree that Margarite was a problem. He might still be alive. Margarite turned him on to cocaine, and I can't forgive her for that. Before he met her, he used weed and good liquor to crack writer's block."

"I'm sorry. That must have been hard to watch."

Ben squeezed her hand. "It was. The shop foreman, Lenny Mishler, had to know what was going on in the Green Room. His shop is next door. Lenny drove Paul crazy, quoting Bible verses and preaching hellfire and damnation. Paul put up with him because Lenny was good at his job. Paul never gave me any reason to believe any faculty knew, though I can't believe they didn't. It's a small department. Just the six of them. Dr. Beckett, his secretary, Sally Featherston, and Lenny. The two professors, Paul and Dr. Knupp, and a guy in the music department, Dale Wilkerson. He works with Paul on the fall musical. Paul's student assistant this term is Roxie Ryland. It's complicated," Ben said with a wry smile. "Roxie broke up with Knupp last year, and Paul was with her maybe three months before he showed her to the door. Roxie went back to Knupp. As far as I know, she's still with him." He shrugged. "I don't think Paul's job was ever in danger, no matter what he did. He was too valuable to the department for them to fire him."

"How did the affair with Roxie affect Paul's work relationship with Knupp?"

"I don't think it did. Paul didn't like Knupp even before Roxie got between them. He thought Knupp was after his job, but the chairman would never let that happen. Dr. Beckett would protect Paul at all costs because of the money Paul brought in."

Ben's eyes were filled with pain. "My brother's weakness was women. He had affairs with his students. There were others before Roxie and Margarite, but he wasn't stealing minors off the street. I kept telling him he shouldn't play in the pool he worked in, but he laughed it off and said everything would be fine. It sounds terrible, and I'm not trying to justify how he acted, but Paul never promised any of these women a forever and forever relationship. He called himself a hedonist, and I think he was pretty upfront about that with the women."

Quinn thought Paul had been more than a hedonist. That he had pressured women to have sex with him. Perhaps Ben didn't know about that part, but she could tell it had cost him to tell her about his brother. There were fine lines of pain around his beautiful eyes and mouth. She reached over and touched his shoulder. "I know talking about Paul is hard."

"No, it's fine. You needed to know." He pushed the hair off his forehead again and smiled. "Enough about me. Do you have family in Denver?"

"My grandparents raised me in the Sunnyside neighborhood. They've passed now, and I have a little bungalow in the Barnum neighborhood and share it with a seventy-pound puppy named Charley."

Ben laughed. "Paul and I brought home a huge stray

dog when we were about ten. He was so hairy I could barely tell one end from the other, but I was crazy about that dog. Mom didn't like him much because he peed on whatever he didn't chew up, but she let us keep him."

Ben had a beautiful smile and was easy to talk to. Quinn wondered what it would feel like to be kissed by those luscious lips. She reminded herself all she could do was admire the view.

"How did you become an investigator?"

"I was a journalist and wrote for a weekly newspaper up in the mountains. I was bored to death. The biggest story I wrote was about a love-sick bull moose trying to mount the bronze statue of a female moose on the village square. The newspaper business gets smaller every year, and I didn't see any future for me. I came back to FRSU and studied criminal justice."

"Good choice."

"What about you? You said you traveled for work. Did you like it?"

"I liked being home in Baltimore on my boat more. I kept it docked at the end of my street."

"Sounds idyllic."

"It was. I traveled to Antwerp and the mines in South Africa and saw most of Europe. The downside was that I had no time for a serious relationship. Until I met a woman at a charity event one night, and everything changed. We were still talking when the sun rose over the Atlantic, and when I drove her home, I knew I was in love. Paul and his wife flew out to meet her, and he dragged me aside and told me to marry her and make babies. That when the noise and fat of life were cut away, a woman and children are all a man has. But it didn't work for us. She wanted a stay-at-home man. I couldn't

give her what she wanted, and she couldn't be satisfied with what I could give her." He looked up at her and seemed embarrassed. "I'm sorry. That was probably way too much information. I'm raw from no sleep, but I shouldn't have shared all that."

"It's fine, really. I talked my friend's ear off after my last breakup. We had no chemistry."

"You have to have the chemistry," he said, smiling. "There's either a spark or not when two people meet, and I'm an unrepentant spark chaser."

Suddenly, she felt awkward. What was she doing blabbing about lost love with a client? Ben was hot, but he also might have murdered his brother. "I better go. I'm keeping you from your customers."

Ben followed her into the hall and touched her arm. "Let me show you how the upstairs is coming along. I hope to move in before summer." He seemed eager to show her the renovations.

What could she say to be polite other than, "Okay."

Ben led the way, turning on work lights as they walked up the stairs to the landing. He stopped in front of a roughed-in door. "The contractor installed the door to keep the cold and dust out of the bar. It's going to be freezing up here." He opened the door to a brisk wind whistling through the stairwell.

Ben put his hand lightly on the small of her back. "Watch your step," he said, following her into a large open space with floor-to-ceiling windows. "There will be two good-sized apartments on this floor, with a great city view. Come on up to the top."

Her teeth chattered as she followed him up the stairs to another floor gutted to the studs. The window frames had plastic sheeting over them, but the wind leaked around the plastic.

"The new windows are delayed," Ben said. Undeterred by the cold, he pointed to where the kitchen would be and where a stone fireplace would be in the living room. His hand lingered on the small of her back. "The sunsets will be gorgeous from up here."

"It's beautiful, but I'm freezing." Quinn backed away. She enjoyed Ben's touch and his company too much. On the way downstairs, she reminded herself that her feelings weren't a problem unless she acted on them.

Ben walked with her through the bar to the front door. "Have dinner with me tomorrow night."

"I don't think that's a good idea, and I'm sure Mr. Meadows wouldn't."

"Okay, let's have a business dinner. We're coworkers. You don't even have to ride with me, though I would enjoy picking you up."

She waffled before saying, "Okay. A business meeting. Where do you want to meet?"

"Angelo's Taverna is the best Italian food in Denver. Seven o'clock. See you there."

Chapter 6

Quinn stopped at her favorite pizzeria to pick up dinner for her and Trixie. The warm smell of cheesy goodness was mouthwatering. She ate too much junk food but hated the measuring, mixing, chopping, and sauteing that home-cooked meals required. It wasn't like she didn't know she could pick up a healthy salad. They sold salads a foot from where she was paying for the pizza. She was simply weak in the knees around Italian food. Someday, she promised herself she'd learn to cook and use her grandmother's notebook full of handwritten recipes, but tonight was another pizza night.

Traffic had thinned by the time she left the restaurant. When she turned onto West Ellsworth, she glanced in the rear-view mirror and saw two men in a large, dark-colored SUV make the turn behind her. When she pulled into her driveway, the vehicle cruised to a stop across the drive, blocking her in. A steady stream of homebound commuters had to veer around the car in the narrow street. Quinn slipped her gun into her waistband, yanked her jacket over it, and marched down the driveway to confront them. No one was going to shoot her in front of the neighbors.

When she was feet from the truck, the driver lowered his window, giving her a good look at his shaved, bullet-shaped head and a nasty scar that zigzagged from the corner of his eye to his chin. "We got a message for you," he growled. "Stay away from the Loughty case."

Before she could respond, he shot away from the curb, cutting in front of a small sedan. The sedan driver braked hard but not fast enough to avoid plowing into the back of the heavy truck. The SUV shot ahead and careened around the corner, leaving the small car stalled in front of her house.

Quinn was still rooted to the spot, staring after the big truck when the sedan driver shouted, "Do you know those guys?"

"No. Are you hurt?"

"But you were talking to them. Look at my car." He crawled out, red-faced and shaking, pointing to the wrecked front end. "This is going to cost a bundle. Did you get the plate number?"

"I'm sorry. I didn't." She'd bet her next paycheck the vehicle was registered to a phony company.

"What's your name? You saw what happened. My insurance company will want to talk to you."

"Quinn Kane." She rattled off her office number. He drove away unhappy with his front bumper scraping the asphalt.

She turned and walked up her driveway. How many people knew she was working on the Loughty case? She hadn't told anyone but Trixie, and Meadows made a living from keeping secrets. Ben had no reason to blab. That narrowed the list to a cop. A cop shop was a hotbed of street gossip, and one detective she knew had something to gain by sowing chaos in the law firm Ben hired.

Quinn unlocked her door, balancing the pizza in one hand. Charley barreled toward her and stopped right before she ran into Quinn's knees and knocked her down. She was trembling and whining. Quinn put the pizza on the counter and wrapped her arms around the dog. "It's okay."

Charley rolled over for a belly scratch, and Quinn wondered why everyone didn't have a good dog to come home to. She put the pizza in the oven to stay warm and poured kibble into Charley's bowl, but the dog wouldn't eat. Instead, Charley stuck by Quinn's side, ears pinned back and whining.

Quinn looked around for what was bothering Charley and noticed the tilted lampshade. The papers on the coffee table weren't where she had left them this morning. Quinn pulled her gun and searched the house. Her closet door was open, and the desk drawers in her office had been rifled. The only thing she had of value was the television, which was still on the table in her living room. Her laptop went to work with her every morning. Nothing was missing, but someone had been inside, done a half-assed, sloppy search, and scared her pup.

She'd changed the locks when she moved in, and no one had a key but Trixie. The weak spot in her security was the sash windows, which were original to the house and hard to close and lock. She would have replaced them if she'd had the cash. No, if she were honest with herself, she would have bought the gorgeous chair she'd seen in the furniture store window.

Quinn circled through the house, checking the window locks, and found the office window open a crack. She snapped it shut and turned the lock. She hadn't left a window open in the dead of winter.

She was still thinking about the intruder when a text

from Truck came through with the name of Bystrom's godfather, Logan Latham.

Truck included the tidbit that Latham's stepdaughter was married to Bystrom's son. Quinn wondered if the family connection was why Latham protected Bystrom. Or was it because Logan Latham was a bigwig in the construction business, and a cop in his pocket came in handy?

She was researching Latham's company's website when she heard a knock at her door. She looked out the peephole to see Trixie finger waving at her.

"Sorry, I'm late," Trixie said. "Coach worked us hard because we were unlucky and drew the Kansas City Rollers for our first match in the Midwest Championships. They beat the crap out of us last year." Trixie headed for the tiny kitchen and put the wine she had brought on the counter. "You can throw me out when you get tired of me. I'm on my own for the evening. Gris took a group skiing in Aspen."

Gris Grissard was Trixie's long-time boyfriend, though there should be another word for a man over forty. They had been together for ten years but kept their separate houses. Trixie called it the perfect solution to the daily grind of living with someone, and it worked for them.

Quinn got two plates out. "Should he be skiing on that ankle?" Gris had taken a nasty fall on the ice, ending his pro hockey career. Now, he was trying to make a living with his guide business. He offered winter ski trips, rock climbing, and white water rafting in the summer, but the economy had taken a toll on his business. It had been slow all summer and fall, and Quinn knew Trixie was worried. The last thing Gris needed was to bust up his ankle again.

"I hope he has sense enough not to get on skis. His clients are all experienced skiers. None of them need him to hold their hands while they ski black diamonds. He could sit in the bar and drink warm toddies, but he's a guy, so who knows what he'll do. Give me the corkscrew, and let's get this party started."

Trixie poured two glasses, and they loaded their plates with pizza and took them to the table. "Who is the new client?"

"Ben Loughty."

"Is he related to the Loughty guy murdered at the college?"

"Twin brother. He hasn't been charged; he wants a lawyer on board."

Trixie swallowed a bite of pizza. "Sounds like he might be worried. What's he like?"

"He's the guy who bought the old hotel on Colfax and opened the Starlight Lounge."

"Uh-huh," Trixie grinned and wiped her hands. "Those are the facts. From the look on your face, he must be something."

Quinn felt silly saying, 'He's gorgeous and charming' even though it was true.

Trixie sipped her wine and made the gimme gesture. "Details, please."

"He could have been a model. Tall, with a flinty jaw, Roman nose, and lips I can't quit thinking about."

"Kissable lips?"

"Absolutely, and expressive gray eyes." Quinn sipped her wine and added, "He did two years for possession with intent when he was young."

"Has he straightened himself out?"

"Looks like it. He was a diamond buyer in Europe before he moved here."

"Sounds romantic," Trixie said.

With a little smile, Quinn added, "He has a touch of European charm from all that travel."

"You have a bad case of man lust!" Trixie said and laughed.

"After five minutes with Ben, any woman would be blind and deaf if she wasn't. But he's a client and strictly hands-off. Besides, I got burned bad when Rick left me. I still have the scorch marks."

Trixie shrugged. "Ben won't always be your client. Do you want that last piece of pizza?"

"All yours."

Trixie helped herself. "Have you ever wondered if you're hiding behind your work instead of getting out there and finding someone?"

"I haven't met the right guy."

"Maybe Ben is the right guy. Do you think he killed his brother?"

"I hope not."

"It would sure put a dent in a romance," Trixie said.

"I'm not sure I'm ready for romance."

"Oh, come on. You've been hibernating for what? Two years? You have to get back in there. Find yourself a guy."

"Maybe after this case is solved."

Trixie heaved an exaggerated sigh. "At least think about finding a guy. So, tell me about the case. Do the cops have evidence against Ben?"

"We won't know what they have until they make an arrest, and maybe not then. Deke Bystrom is the lead detective."

"That's not good. You never told me the whole story of what happened between you two."

Quinn shuddered and squeezed her eyes shut, wishing she could forget. "That was the worst case of my career. A woman named Suze Nelson was arrested for prostitution. She made her one phone call from lockup to Deke Bystrom. She begged him to fix the charges against her. Of course, the jailers were listening, and Bystrom knew it, so he acted like he didn't know who she was. The following day, her roommate bailed her out. Suze got her revenge. She sent pornographic pictures of her and Bystrom doing the deed to the District Attorney. Suze claimed Bystrom was one of her regulars. Of course, Bystrom claimed he didn't know she was a prostitute and never paid her a dime."

"Yeah, right." Trixie refilled their glasses. "Totally believable."

"The D.A. didn't have to decide if Bystrom was lying because Suze surprised everyone and recanted her story. She took the stand and testified it was a lover's spat between her and Bystrom, and no money ever changed hands. Her roommate pulled me aside and told me she'd heard Bystrom threaten to take Suze's two minor children from her unless she claimed they were lovers. I passed that on to the District Attorney. He put the roommate on the stand, and she told the jury that Bystrom had threatened Suze."

"So, Suze beat the rap?"

Quinn waved the idea away. "No, someone put the fix in, and the jury found her guilty. But, the roommate's testimony triggered an Internal Affairs investigation. Eventually, Bystrom skated on that, but his reputation took a beating. He knows I pushed the roommate to testify against him, and he threatened to get even."

"Wow, that case had it all: prostitution, revenge, and witness tampering. He sounds like a real sweetheart," Trixie said.

"Oh, he is. He's filed a complaint against me with the State Board, claiming I represented myself as a cop when I talked to Paul Loughty's girlfriend. I'm more worried about Meadows. I could lose my job. Meadows fires anyone who hurts the reputation of the firm. I've heard him say more than once that our clients come to us because of our good name. I'm skating on thin ice."

"How are you going to handle that?"

"Work like crazy to convince Meadows I'm worth keeping."

"You need to get a lawyer on board," Trixie advised.

"I'm dragging my heels because of what it will cost. I don't think Margarite recorded the interview, but if she did, Bystrom could take the recording to an audio expert. A text-to-speech Artificial Intelligence tool can clone a voice with only a three-second audio sample. A line of conversation could be inserted into the interview with me claiming I'm a cop. If that happens, I'll have to fork over the money for a lawyer and a forensic expert to review the tape."

"That sounds too pricey for Bystrom to do on a detective's salary, not to mention too technical for the old fart."

"It might not cost Bystrom a dime. Logan Latham is his godfather."

Trixie squinted at her over her glass. "No kidding."

"Truck told me, and he's never wrong. Look at this." Quinn picked up her phone and pulled up the Latham Construction website. "His construction company specializes in building homes for the rich and famous. Look at the pictures of houses he built in Vail and Aspen." Quinn handed her phone to Trixie.

"I don't like that ultra-modern stuff. They look like spaceships clinging to the mountainside." She finished the last piece of pizza. "I've heard about Latham from work. He has a multi-million-dollar home overlooking Wash Park, a mountain home near Vail, and, wait for it, a home in Fiji. He's a car collector, too, and probably has a trophy wife who wears mink."

"I thought wearing a mink wrap was considered barbaric now," Quinn said. Trixie worked for a company good enough at finding secrets to have a contract with the Department of Defense. "What was Latham into that caught your eye?"

"Construction fraud," Trixie said.

"Tell me about it."

"Latham's company had a contract to build runways at a regional airport in Eastern Kansas. He billed for high-end material, bought the cheap stuff, and pocketed the money. Then he bribed an inspector to certify the runways met the FAA standards." Trixie licked her finger to get the last pizza crumbs off her plate. "That's not all. Latham and a rival CEO were ordered to mediation to resolve their differences. The mediator decided in Latham's favor, and the lawyer who represented the opposing company complained to the judge that there was an unusual amount of interference in the process by a Denver police detective. Guess who it was?"

"Bystrom," Quinn said. "What did he do?"

"The judge issued a gag order. No one is talking."

"I think Bystrom feeds Latham confidential

information, and Latham uses his considerable influence and money to keep Bystrom on the job."

"Sounds about right, and they are both dangerous," Trixie said.

Quinn nodded. "Two goons in a dark SUV followed me home and warned me off the case. Plus, someone was in my house before I got home. Stuff had been moved around, and Charley wouldn't let me out of her sight."

"Was anything stolen?"

"Not that I can tell."

"Maybe instead of taking something *out*," Trixie offered, "they put something *into* your house, like a camera or listening device. I have an electronic gizmo we can scan it with. Give me a minute."

After Trixie left, Quinn went to lock the door. Then, feeling it was overkill, she left it open. In less than five minutes, Trixie returned with a small plastic box. She swept through the house, and the device never made a sound. Trixie plopped down in a chair. "The place is clean. You'll call me if you need me, right?"

Quinn nodded. Her brain was working overtime. She needed evidence linking Latham and Bystrom, but she had another job to do tonight before the bar closed, and Ben went home.

"Am I keeping you from something?" Trixie asked.

"I have one more job to do tonight."

"At this hour?"

"I'm going to have a look inside Ben's house. My old psych professor said if you want to know someone, get inside their home and see how they live. I was so uptight I didn't take a date back to my apartment for months."

Trixie sat back and grinned. "Reminds me of the

work I did as an Intelligence officer. It would have never passed the smell test outside the Army, but it was very effective." She put her wine glass in the sink and headed for the door. "Hey, let me know if you find a negligee stuffed under Ben's pillow."

Chapter 7

After Trixie left, Quinn changed into black pants and stuffed her hair under a dark watch cap. She coaxed Charley into the backyard, and while the puppy hunted for the perfect spot to relieve herself, Quinn used her burner phone to call the Starlight Lounge. Since Ben's nephew would arrive tomorrow, this might be the last evening she could safely search his home.

Her call was routed to Ben's office, and when he answered, she hung up, satisfied he was at work. Charley ran into the house and plopped her butt down at Quinn's feet. She knew Quinn was dressed to leave and gave off her mournful 'don't leave me' look. "You can't go this time. Bed."

Charley trotted off to her bed. Her sad eyes followed Quinn to the front door to ensure her owner would feel guilty on the way out.

Quinn trudged across the snowy yard to her car. With a bitterly cold wind and heavy snow clouds hiding the sky in a drapery of velvety black, sensible people were inside and enjoying a drink by a crackling fire. Quinn hoped Ben's neighbors were tucked in for the night and that he didn't have a doorbell camera.

All she knew about Ben was the little she'd found online and what he had told her. Ben might be something other than eye candy and charming. Tonight, she was taking her grandfather's advice to heart.

He was a history buff and had taken her to the Little Big Horn battlefield. When they stood on Last Stand Hill, he pointed to the gravestones and said, *it's what you don't know that you don't know, that will bite you in the arse every time*. She'd had some painful experiences with ignorance and didn't want a repeat.

Quinn cruised past the Jefferson Condominiums, which looked nothing like their namesake. It was a tall, narrow building crowded between two skyscrapers. She parked a block away and walked back with her head tucked low to ward off the lash of the wind. She willed herself to quit worrying about the complaint to her licensure board and what Meadows might do. She needed to concentrate on getting in and out of Ben's home without being caught.

She slipped inside the controlled access door behind an elderly man returning from walking his dog. While the dog walker waited for the elevator, Quinn entered the mailroom and checked the mailboxes. The building had five floors, with four apartments on each floor. With twenty units and a communal mailroom, the building was small enough for the tenants to notice a stranger roaming the building at night. She'd have to be quick and careful.

She waited until the elevator rose and then took the stairs to Ben's corner apartment on the top floor. She was bent over and working her lock picks when the elevator dinged. She shoved the lockpick into her pocket and walked the hall, trying to look like a visitor hunting for the right apartment.

When the elevator door whooshed open, Quinn half-turned and saw it was empty. She returned to Ben's door. After three nerve-wracking tries, working first one pick, then another, and worrying a neighbor would pop into the hall, waving a cell phone and threatening to call the police, the tumblers shifted. The knob turned smoothly, and she was inside. Quinn studied the walls and ceilings for signs of a camera feeding footage of her break-in to Ben's cell phone. She relaxed when she saw no signs of surveillance.

Her first impression was that everything was expensive and went together—nothing like her home, where each piece came from a yard sale or a second-hand store. The room was masculine, with a luxurious black leather sofa flanked by two matching chairs, an ebony bookcase with more sculptures than books, and a single bold abstract painting over the fireplace. The living area had a large west-facing window providing a stunning view of the Denver skyline like he would have in his home on the third floor of the Starlight.

Ben had no personal photos, clutter, or even junk mail. The room was beautiful but sterile, and it could have been a display in a furniture store. She thought of the homey clutter in her home. Things from her grandparents' house. Vintage odds and ends she'd picked up at the flea market. Maybe she just thought it all worked together, and really, it was an eyesore. It was certainly hard to keep dusted.

She made quick work of searching the living room and found nothing unusual. She headed to his bedroom, where she found a king-size bed neatly made with a black and gray comforter. The only other furniture was a single nightstand and a chest of drawers. Inside the matching chest, Quinn found neatly folded t-shirts, socks, and underwear in neat stacks. She moved into the closet and found his clothes arranged by color and type.

Some had tags from a tailor in London. She pulled a matching set of leather suitcases off the closet shelf, ran her hand around the inside lining, searched for a false bottom, and found nothing. She knew nothing about men's shoes, but Ben's looked expensive. He didn't own a closet full of clothes, but he had the best quality. Most of his shirts were cut alike and white or pale blue. Everything on the bathroom shelves was precisely aligned. Ben liked order. Before heading to the kitchen, she checked to see that she had left the bedroom and bath as tidy as she had found it.

One look in Ben's refrigerator, and she knew he ate out far more than he cooked. He had the usual kitchen gadgets, but he wasn't entertaining with only two place settings of pottery. She searched through his meager food stash in the pantry and took everything out from under the sink, a place Mr. Tidy hadn't cleaned in a while. Finally, she climbed on top of the quartz countertops, stretched her arm up, and ran her hand across the tops of the cabinets. Her fingers closed around a metal clip. She pulled a dusty brown envelope from the space between two units and dumped the contacts on the counter. Three passports tumbled out, each with Ben's picture but a different name. There were credit cards to match each of his identities.

She stared at them in disbelief. She didn't want to believe what she saw. Ben could assume any of these identities and disappear anywhere in the world. He was probably laughing at how easily he'd fooled her, the hometown girl with few experiences. But he hadn't played straight with Meadows either, and whatever Ben had done while using the false identities could torpedo Meadows' defense.

She had been a fool to think she and Ben could have a relationship. She had let her heart race out of the gate before her brain reached the starting line, but her record with men was depressing. One relationship died of boredom, and another was to a man fifteen years her senior who was tied to his ex-wife in ways neither she nor he understood. Then, there was her last lover. Rick, the hot guy who waltzed out the door, telling her no one would ever love her as much as he did. She'd turned that into a self-fulfilling prophecy and been a hermit for two years. Maybe Trixie was right. There was someone out there who would love her more than Rick. She just needed to find him because it wasn't Ben Loughty.

She stuffed the documents in the holder and hung them where she found them. Cold and logical now, she knew a man as precise as Ben had to have cash hidden in the house. He couldn't run far without money, and probably half a dozen burner phones were in the house, too.

She looked in all the easy places before she sat on the kitchen floor and inspected the kickboards beneath the cabinets. The kickboard's job was to keep the cook from hanging her foot up in the space under the cabinets. Behind the board was an area the same width and length as the unit and a couple of inches high. An excellent hiding place.

Quinn scooted across the floor, tapping one board, then another, looking for one that sounded different. She found a kickboard slightly askew, popped off the quarter-round trim, and yanked off the kickboard. It had been held in place with double-sided sticky tape. She trained a penlight under the cabinet, hoping she didn't find a nest of mice or a giant hairy spider. There wasn't room for even one skinny mouse.

She hauled out a metal case and flipped the latches. Inside were crisp one-hundred-dollar bills, with the paper ring still around them. She had found his stash. Ben could grab the case, his fake passports and credit cards, and hop a plane to anywhere in the world, like the remote island off the coast of Brazil. Maybe instead of fishing, Ben had hidden there and enjoyed the beautiful women while the cops hunted him for whatever crime he committed that netted him the money.

She shoved the case under the cabinet, lined up the kickboard, and stuck it into place. She better get out before Ben returned or a neighbor heard a noise coming from his apartment. At the front door, Quinn looked through the peephole. The hall was empty. She let herself out and hurried down the stairs. She thought she was home free until she reached the door from the stairwell into the foyer. Someone in the lobby was singing off-key at the top of his lungs.

A drunk man shoved his access card in and out of the elevator's control slot. He jerked it out and looked at the offending card like the plastic was the problem. He tried again, and when the door didn't open, he lurched toward the stairwell.

Lucky for her, the elevator door sounded a tone and opened. He was wobbly on his feet and nearly stumbled, but he managed to stay upright long enough to thrust his arm inside the door to keep it open. He climbed in, and the door slid shut.

Quinn breathed a sigh of relief and hung back until she saw the numbers rising. Then she hurried out of the building, hoping she didn't look like a fleeing burglar.

Back in her car, she thought her psychology

professor was spot on. Fake passports, credit cards, and a hoard of money weren't signs of a man making a fresh start like Ben claimed. They were what a man on the run used. She decided she would let Ben think that she believed everything he told her. She would wait for him to make a mistake. She could play games, too, and everyone eventually slipped up. Quinn was exhausted when she pulled into the driveway.

She checked the bottom panel of the front door for the strip of cellphone tape she'd left across the door frame. It was still in place. No one had been inside while she was gone. Before she went to bed, she double-checked the doors and windows.

Ben weaved in and out of dreams, always hovering on the edges of her vision. She finally gave up trying to sleep and got up to a bone-chilling Tuesday morning. She dressed quickly and fed Charley before downing a cup of coffee and a granola bar while standing over the kitchen sink.

Twenty-four hours had passed since Paul Loughty's murder, and she had no leads.

Chapter 8

Quinn crossed through the sky bridge to the law firm. She knew she should go directly to her office and call Ben to cancel their dinner date, but she stopped in the staff room to check her mail. She flipped through the various envelopes and stopped when she found an envelope from Doc Iverson, the county's brilliant forensic pathologist. She had an understanding with Doc. He passed her information in return for a steady supply of Cuban cigars. She had no idea how Truck smuggled the cigars out of Cuba, and she slept better, not knowing. She stuffed the rest of the mail into her bag and ripped open the note. By the time she'd finished reading Iverson's summary of Paul Loughty's autopsy, Meadows had stuck his head in the door. He looked tired and disheveled.

"A minute, Quinn?"

"Sure." She followed him to his office, hoping Bystrom hadn't made more trouble.

Meadows started talking before she sat down. "Bystrom pulled Ben in last night and told him he had evidence that Ben killed his brother. He told him to confess, and things would go easier for him. Even hinted Ben might be able to get a plea deal if he came clean."

No wonder Ben hadn't walked in on her while she searched his home last night.

"Bystrom was lying to us," Meadows said. He

wanted to wring a confession out of Ben and clear the case. I asked him to produce an arrest warrant signed by a judge, and he didn't have one. I told him we were leaving and took Ben home."

Quinn thought about what she found in Ben's kitchen last night. "How is he holding up?"

Meadows' phone pinged. He glanced at it and flipped it over. "He was shaken last night, but I think he'll stay strong. He and Jason are having Paul's celebration of life later this week at the bar, so hold your evenings free. Did you find a decent alibi for him?"

Quinn knew her boss wasn't going to like her answer. "None of his neighbors heard or saw him Sunday evening."

"That's not good," Meadows said. "I don't have his cell phone records yet. Let's hope his cell pinged off a tower by his home all night, though it would only prove the phone stayed home."

Quinn didn't know how to sugarcoat what she had discovered. "He has multiple passports in different names, all with the same picture, credit cards for each identity, and plenty of cash."

Meadows tapped a rhythm on his desk with his fingers, something he did when thinking. She knew he wouldn't ask her how she got the information. It was part of their game to keep his plausible deniability in place.

"Lots of people keep cash around, and owning fake identities isn't illegal. Using them to commit a crime is. Do you have any evidence he's committed a crime under another name?"

"No, but he has an offshore account in the Caymans. He looks ready to leave the country if he's arrested."

Meadows frowned. "Our job is to see to it that our

client doesn't think he has to make a run for it in the middle of the night. The offshore money doesn't raise any red flags for me. Let's say Ben was involved in something illegal that earned him the money he put offshore. If the illegal activity isn't related to Paul's murder, it has no bearing on this case. Is there any proof there's a connection between Paul's murder and the money?"

"Not that I've found."

Looking satisfied, Meadows nodded. "Good. Don't look real hard."

Quinn wasn't as confident about Ben's hidden cache as Meadows, but she wasn't thinking like a lawyer. She was judging Ben's character, and he was coming up short. She couldn't believe she'd thought he might be her one-man-drought buster.

Quinn moved on to other business. "I have Doc Iverson's autopsy notes. You want the short version?"

Meadows nodded.

"The time of death was between seven and ten on Sunday night, and he was shot at close range while he sat on the sofa."

"It sounds like Paul knew his killer," Meadows said.

"Yes, I think so, too. Doc didn't find any defensive wounds on Paul, only a few faded bruises on his right shin. He let his killer get close. The tox screen showed he was legally intoxicated, and he had a trace amount of cocaine in his system—but Doc says Paul wasn't so impaired that he couldn't have stood and defended himself."

Meadows raised his eyebrows. "The drugs in Paul's system could be a problem for Ben. He'd better be as clean as he claims. What kind of gun was used?"

"A twenty-two-caliber pistol, loaded with hollow points. Iverson told me the police hadn't found the gun, and the bullets didn't match any database."

"The killer probably bought the gun off the street and has sold it to someone else. Did Iverson give an opinion on the blood trail on the floor? He's the blood expert."

"Nothing yet."

"Something odd about that blood trail on the floor," Meadows said. "Take a look at these." He turned his computer screen around so Quinn could see. "These aren't all the pictures taken at the crime scene, only the ones my source would share. It could be that the pictures I'm not seeing are more important than what we're looking at."

"I'll go to the theater today, take pictures, and talk to Paul's colleagues." Quinn hoped Bystrom's crime techs were finished. The chances that Bystrom would let her anywhere near his crime scene were slim and none.

Meadows pointed to the picture of Paul's body slumped over on his side on one end of the sofa. Quinn scooted forward in the chair to see the monitor better. A partially eaten sandwich was on the floor by the body, and an open bottle of an excellent single malt whiskey stood half empty on the coffee table.

"Look at the blood trail on the floor. The drops start at the threshold and end near the sofa. I requested a blood sample from the crime scene and sent Ben to a doctor for a physical exam. He found no scratches or open wounds on Ben."

"That's good news," Quinn said.

"Hope so. We'll know soon enough if we have a problem. I had the doctor take blood from Ben and send

66

it and blood samples from the scene to the Bharat Lab this morning. Since that story broke about the cop lab leaving samples on the counter overnight and broken refrigerators, no sane defense attorney would accept their results. I'm not jeopardizing Ben's future over a dodgy lab report from the cops."

"If Ben killed Paul, he would know about the blood on the floor. That he agreed to be examined by the doctor and have his blood drawn means Ben knew his blood wouldn't match blood from the scene."

"I hope he's that smart." Meadows put his palms flat on his desk. "Don't waste a lot of time searching for an alibi for Ben. He would have told us by now if he had a good one. I need you to find someone who had a motive to kill Paul and access to the theater. I can sow reasonable doubt in a jury's mind that someone other than Ben had the opportunity and a reason to kill Paul. Jurors want an airtight case before they send a man down for murder. They don't want to be second-guessing themselves as the bailiff marches the defendant out of the courtroom."

Quinn thought about talking with Meadows about Logan Latham but shied away from bringing it up. Meadows preferred facts to theories, and he'd just doubled down on her workload. She had to find someone to hang the murder on so Meadows could defend Ben with the reasonable doubt argument. Quinn had no choice but to say, "I'll find someone," and hoped she could. She stood to leave.

Meadows waved her back to her seat. His mouth drew down in a frown. "Have you gotten a lawyer to represent you before the state board? As much as I appreciate your work—and I surely do—our clients come to us because of our reputation. A single incident can erase years of impeccable work. Don't disappoint me, Quinn."

"I'll get on that today."

"It should already be done. Don't lose control of the situation." He shot his cuffs and looked at his watch. The meeting was officially over.

Quinn walked out, thinking it was a good thing Meadows didn't know about the visitors at her house last night. She slipped into her office and closed the door.

Quinn shuffled through the rest of her mail and found a registered letter from her bank with a sticky note from the receptionist on the envelope saying she had signed for it late yesterday. Quinn ripped it open to find that her home loan had been sold to another bank. She didn't recognize the name of the new lien holder, but she didn't think much about it. The loan had been sold before. She wondered why they went to the trouble of sending a certified letter and set it aside to take home and file with her mortgage papers.

Under the last piece of junk mail was a letter from a bank she wasn't familiar with. She was breathing like a racehorse as she read that the new lien holder was calling her loan due. She had to pay the balance in thirty days, or the house would go into foreclosure.

Quinn was rooted to the spot. There was no way she could pay off the loan, and if she lost her house, it would take years for her to claw her way back to having a good enough credit rating to own a home. If she lost her license, she'd never do it.

Tears welled in her eyes. When her grandmother died, she used the money from the sale of her home for a down payment on her little house. If the bank took her home, she would lose the last gift her grandmother had given her. A fresh wave of pain rolled over her when she realized she could lose her job over the foreclosure. The firm ran regular credit checks on all the staff. Meadows would find out about her financial problems. Everything she held dear was being stripped away: her reputation, job, and home.

She straightened her shoulders. There was no upside in moping and whining; she never folded without a fight.

She called Ed Adams, a lawyer who had taught a seminar she attended. They had even dated casually before moving on. The call went to voice mail, and she didn't leave a message because she wasn't sure if Ed's secretary screened his messages. The fewer people who knew what was happening to her, the better. She hung up and dialed Truck.

"I thought you'd be calling. I have nothing you'll be happy to hear on the Loughty case. The cop shop is locked down tighter than a drum. No one is gossiping, and that's unusual."

Quinn really didn't care about that right now. "Who owns Grand Summit Bank?"

"Logan Latham. Why?"

Crap, how could this be happening. "Latham bought my home loan and is foreclosing if I don't pay the balance on the loan."

"Sounds like him. Rember the Nelson case?"

How could she forget?

"Latham hired guys to dig up dirt on the jury members. That's why they voted Suze guilty."

Quinn fumed. Truck should have told her that at the time, but that wasn't his way. Truck was stingy about sharing information. "Losing the house isn't my only problem. Bystrom's complained to my licensing board that I impersonated a cop."

"Bystrom's a screwup. He'd run outside with a fork if it were raining soup but watch your back. Latham's the brains, and he calls the shots. Three years ago, Bystrom took a gun from the police evidence locker and passed it to Latham. One of Latham's competitors was killed with it."

"Thanks for the heads up," Quinn said.

"Take it seriously. Don't worry about the bank. I'll loan you the money to pay off your loan, and if I can help with the license problem, you know I will."

Quinn was nervous about borrowing money from Truck. She knew how he earned it and didn't need the problems that borrowing from him might bring. "I need a place to live. Do you still have those apartment buildings?"

"Yeah, I'll find a unit for you to move into. When do you need it?"

"I don't know. How long does foreclosure take?"

"If it's a legitimate bank, it could take months, but Latham will bully it through as fast as possible. You need to get out of the house as soon as you can. If he forecloses and you're not out, he could keep your stuff against the unpaid loan."

The bad news never ended. While she didn't have much, she owned it. "All right. I'll look for someone to help me move."

"Babe, when you're ready to move, I'll send over two of my guys and a truck for free."

"Thank you." She hated feeling indebted.

"Don't worry about paying the rent on time. I know you're good for the money. What else do you need?"

"Evidence that Latham and Bystrom are scratching each other's backs. Found any?"

"Nothing that you can take to the D.A."

Chapter 9

Quinn needed to leave her office and do something productive—like solve Paul Loughty's murder. She couldn't just stew the rest of the day over Latham's ultimatum. But first, she had to call Ben. It wouldn't get easier to tell him she wasn't having dinner with him, and she didn't want to spend the morning dreading the call.

On the third ring, Ben picked up. "Hi, Quinn," he said in that bone-warming voice. "I made us a reservation for tonight at Angelo's, and I'm looking forward to our evening together."

Quinn wanted to tell him she thought he was a slick criminal with fake passports and a wad of cash but choked back the words. "I'm sorry I can't make it."

"Is anything wrong?"

"No, I have to work."

"Okay," he said hesitantly. "If anything were wrong, you would tell me, right?"

"Everything is fine." It was one of those white lies she said to stop a conversation from spiraling into hell. She wasn't ready to confront Ben with what she'd discovered.

"I'm sorry, too," he said. "Maybe we can reschedule soon."

Quinn didn't remember who said what to end the conversation. She was glad it was over and had no intention of going out with him.

She left the office to talk with Paul's colleagues at the college and hoped Ben wouldn't complain to Meadows that she was leaving him out in the cold. She had explained to Ben there would be interviews she had to do alone, and he better get used to it. Today wouldn't be the only time she left him at the curb.

Quinn knew the neighborhood around the Denver Arts College well. The school was across Speer Boulevard from Front Range State University, a public university with twenty-five thousand students and a dazzling array of majors and programs. In contrast, DAC had fewer than three thousand students, was private and expensive, and encouraged their students to be engines of social change. Most of the students she'd known at FRSU were like her, scurrying between classes and work, too exhausted to think much about changing anything.

As she drove by, she saw students circle the parking lots in their cars like hawks hunting prey. On-campus parking was still as limited as when she'd been in school. She stopped at a light and watched students cross the street with their heads down, scrolling through their phones and oblivious to traffic. She felt old. In her day, a phrase she knew made her sound ancient; she and her friends talked as they crossed campus. Now, everyone was in their personal digital silo, and it didn't look like nearly as much fun.

She turned north on Larimer Street and followed the DAC campus signs to the Alderberry Theater. When she couldn't find a visitor's lot, she left her car in a student lot adjacent to the theater. She scribbled *visitor* on a scrap of paper and left it on the dashboard. She hiked up her bag and walked away, remembering from her college days how free campus cops could be with parking tickets.

The Arts College would have looked at home in New England. Red brick buildings with white columns surrounded a commons area studded with large trees. Flower beds rested under a blanket of deep snow. There was even a white chapel with a steeple and a bell tower. A wide sidewalk lined with light poles hung with colorful flags ran through the middle of campus. Quinn stopped at a touchscreen map and found the drama department was next door to the theater. As she passed the Alderberry Theater, an icy wind whipped the yellow crime scene tape. She turned her collar up and jammed her hands in her pockets. Quinn knew she would have to talk her way into the theater.

The department had a suite of offices on the first floor of the building. Five professional photographs of the faculty and staff hung on the wall beside the door, each with their name, title, and office number under the picture. Someone had placed a wreath around Paul's image.

Quinn hadn't made appointments to talk with Paul's colleagues. If she caught them off guard, they would be more likely to share information they wouldn't have if they'd had time to think about it.

She entered an airy reception area with plenty of chairs and copies of *American Theater Magazine* on a small table. A Christmas tree with red lights and tiny silver bells leaned in one corner, looking much like Charlie Brown's sad tree.

A woman sat behind the reception desk, having an animated phone conversation. She looked at Quinn and motioned for her to take a chair. Her iron-gray hair was swept into a dramatic French twist, held in place by a gold comb, and long gold earrings swept her shoulders. Behind her desk was a workroom with several computers and shelves full of books. Sally's desk sat between a hall that led to faculty offices and a large corner office with a nameplate identifying it as belonging to Henry Beckett, Ph.D.

A young woman, probably a student by the look of her, was sitting in a chair, thumbing through her phone and looking impatient.

The receptionist ended her call and said to Quinn, "I'm Sally Featherston. Sorry about the wait. The phone's been ringing off the wall today, just like Monday. How can I help you?"

Quinn identified herself as an investigator working on Dr. Loughty's case. "Is Dr. Beckett available?"

"He's in a meeting with the dean at the moment."

"I can't wait any longer," the young woman said. "I have stuff to do."

Sally told her, "I'll tell Dr. Beckett you stopped by." Sally watched the girl leave and said to Quinn, "Kids, these days, can't sit and wait fifteen minutes."

Quinn smiled. "Seems like it. Do you have time to answer a few questions?"

"Sure, I'm not getting any work done. That dang phone won't quit ringing. I've worked here for over twenty years, longer than anyone else. I know what goes on here. Ask away."

"I never had the pleasure of meeting Dr. Loughty. I'm trying to get to know him."

Sally pointed to the hallway. "Did you see the flowers in the hall where the faculty offices are? That's Prof Paul's office. Students have been bringing them, and I've already had to clean them up once this morning because they were blocking the hall. The students loved him, and they'll miss him something terrible. He did everything to help them. Got them into summer stock and helped them get internships and jobs. He was the one that students loved. But," Sally said as a frown crossed her face. "Someone will tell you this, so you might as well hear it from me." She leaned forward like she was talking to a co-conspirator. "I can't believe educated people could act like they do. The backstabbing, and oh my God, the spitefulness."

"What was the problem?"

"Mostly, it's jealousy," she said. "We're a small department." Sally gave the same description as Ben of Paul's workplace. "Dr. Knupp and Prof Paul teach the classes and direct the plays, and Dr. Beckett runs the place. Lenny Mishler and I are the staff. He runs the scene shop. Poor guy found Paul's body. Did you know Lenny had a heart attack and is in the hospital?" She didn't wait for Quinn to answer. "Anyway, he's going to be okay. Where was I? Oh, yeah, no one can take a toot in this place without everyone knowing. Dr. Beckett wasn't going to fire Paul, no matter what anyone said was happening. I didn't believe a word of it anyway."

Quinn noticed that Sally called the other professors by their academic titles, but Dr. Loughty was 'Prof Paul.' Did he encourage the familiarity of her pet name for him, or was she smitten with him? "What happened?"

"Oh, one student got her knickers in a weenie-wad and filed a lawsuit, but I don't think anything really happened to her."

"It sounds like it could be unpleasant to work here."

A noisy group of students passed by outside. One

young man opened the door and said to Sally, "Sorry to hear about Dr. Loughty."

"Thank you. We'll all miss him," Sally called to him.

When the students were out of earshot, Sally said, "It got real ugly. Me and Lenny stayed because we got our retirements to think about. Mostly, it was Dr. Knupp griping, but Dr. Wilkerson said his piece, too. They accused Paul of some nasty stuff."

"Did they have any evidence?"

"No, they were just green-eyed monsters. They wanted Dr. Beckett to fire Paul." Sally cocked her head toward Dr. Beckett's office. "I heard them accuse Paul of using drugs." Sally leaned forward and lowered her voice. "And having sex with students. Vile stuff. Prof Paul was just friendly, that's all. And I don't think he was doing drugs. They hated Paul because he was so talented. He could direct, write, and bring in the money. Paul got Marvin Alderberry's widow to donate the money for the new theater and plenty of other donations. Dr. Beckett rewarded him with a bigger budget for his productions. Seems fair to me. We would have dried up and blown away without the money Paul brought in. Do you know how few students major in drama these days? No one comes to college to get an education. The kids want to become hedge fund managers or computer wizards. It's like colleges have become vocational schools. Anyway," she said as she threw up her hands in a show of frustration. "Sorry, it's a pet peeve of mine. You need to know that Prof Paul saved the theater program, and the rest of the faculty couldn't stand him. They should have been kissing his tushy."

Sally's phone rang again. "That dang phone. Why

can't people leave us in peace?" She picked it up, listened momentarily, then said, "I'm not talking about Dr. Loughty, and don't call again."

"I see you are busy," Quinn murmured. "I have one more question."

Cocking her head, Sally smiled. "You're going to ask me where I was on Sunday night. It's just like on TV. The cops asked me the same question. I was playing Bunko at Rhea's house. That's Dr. Knupp's wife. A group of us girls plays every Sunday night."

"Great, thanks."

A sudden gust of wind rattled the windows. A crack of thunder boomed, and a jagged slash of lightning streaked across the sky. Sally craned her neck for a better look. "I hope I get to leave early. This storm is going to be a doozy."

"Sounds like a plan. Is it all right with you if I wait here for Dr. Beckett?"

"Help yourself. I have to email the cast and crew to let them know rehearsals are canceled until Dr. Beckett can get someone else to direct the play." She swiveled her chair around to her computer.

Quinn was checking her phone, looking for a message from Ed Adams, when a man in his late fifties, thin and long-limbed, came into the office. "Afternoon, Sally."

"Hi, Dr. Beckett," Sally turned and gave him a thousand-watt smile. "You have someone waiting to see you."

Quinn introduced herself and said, "Can you spare me a few minutes?"

Dr. Beckett motioned her into his office. "Certainly. Come in. What can I do for you?"

She sat across from him, thinking he looked like Ichabod Crane with a goatee. "I'm with the Meadows Law Firm. Dr. Loughty is our client."

Beckett's face turned sour. "Is Paul's family planning to sue the college?"

"Not that I know of." She understood where he was coming from. He already had one lawsuit involving Paul hanging over his head.

Beckett fiddled with the papers on his desk, then cleared his throat. "I've worked with Paul for years. He was a talented director and an accomplished playwright. He even directed one of his original works on Broadway. All of us in the department will miss him."

It sounded rehearsed to Quinn. "I never had the pleasure of meeting him. He sounds very talented. What was it like working with him?"

"Paul was a professional through and through. His work kept the department afloat. The Alderberry Theater is a showplace our slim budget couldn't have afforded. Paul raised the money from a donor. The theater attracts students, and they love training in the facility. He was also our best recruiter. Paul visited high school theater programs all over the country and offered scholarships to the most talented students. You see, we need every student we can get. We're a small department, and the pencil pushers want to eliminate us and put the money into the departments with more majors. It's not just drama under the ax. It's any department that's not adding majors each year. It won't be a college if we lose the liberal and fine arts disciplines. We'll turn into some glorified trade school. I'll be training kids to be carpenters, not thespians."

"So, Paul's work was vital for everyone in the

department, even Sally and the shop foreman."

"Absolutely. We are hard-working professionals who collaborate to make this department successful." Beckett shook his head. "Poor Lenny. He's near retirement age, and he isn't going to be able to return to work after the heart attack. I'll have another position to fill." He sipped from a mug of coffee, made a face, and pushed it to one side. "Please extend our condolences to Ben on the loss of his brother. Will there be a service for Paul?"

"I understand there will be a celebration of Paul's life one evening this week. I'll call your office when I know the date. Do you know Ben well?"

"Not really. He seemed very pleasant the few times I talked with him. I admire the preservation work he's doing downtown." He glanced pointedly at the clock on his desk.

"Who will become the new director of theater?" Quinn asked, not ready to leave.

"I don't know if the college will keep funding Paul's position. One of the ways to kill a struggling department is to cut faculty positions. I've recommended Dr. Knupp for the job, and I'm waiting to see what the college will do. If the position is funded, I can hire him this week."

"You're making it sound like it would be career suicide for anyone associated with the department to have killed Dr. Loughty."

He blanched. "I can't imagine anyone here killing him. The murderer has to be an outsider. There's a homeless camp in the woods behind the theater. They've been a pestilence, sneaking into the theater to sleep and stealing everything, even the toilet paper. Last summer, a homeless man mugged one of our students at a sandwich shop on campus. One of them could have murdered Paul. I hope they tear that camp down and move those awful people."

He cleared his throat and looked nervous. "I'm sorry. I didn't mean to sound insensitive to the homeless. I, uh, am troubled by the ramifications of Paul's death. Perhaps you can help me. One of our best student's mothers called this morning to tell me she is pulling her daughter out of the school because of the murder. If you could fast-track your investigation and find the killer, we can put this terrible time behind us and move on."

"Dr. Beckett, we are giving the case our full attention."

"Of course, thank you," he stammered. "It's just so hard to believe he's gone."

"Were you aware that Dr. Loughty used drugs?"

Dr. Beckett flinched. "The Denver Arts College has a zero-tolerance policy on drugs. To my knowledge, there is no drug use in the theater. Now," he said, shuffling papers on his desk, "I have another appointment."

"Of course. Thank you for your time. One more question. Where were you the night Paul died?"

"I was home with my wife, watching TV." He answered like a man who knew the question was coming and was prepared. Dr. Beckett was reaching for his phone as she walked out.

Quinn returned to Sally's desk. "Do you know when Dr. Knupp will be in his office?"

Sally looked at the clock on her desk. "He should be on his way back from class. His office is the second one down the hall, next to Paul's. Hmmm." She looked flustered. "Sorry, it's hard to believe he's not coming back."

"Thank you. I might get some coffee while I wait." Quinn wanted to talk with Dr. Knupp far from Sally's big ears. She remembered passing a lounge area near the front of the building. From there, she'd see Dr. Knupp as he approached and coax him to talk with her there.

Quinn sat in the empty lounge facing the windows and gathered her thoughts about what she'd learned. Sally had been gossipy and garrulous, describing a toxic workplace fired by jealousy and resentment. Since Dr. Beckett needed his rainmaker to keep the department afloat, Quinn couldn't think of any advantage to him from Paul's death. Beckett's wife provided her husband with an alibi. Still, it was questionable because a wife couldn't be forced to testify against her husband.

Dr. Knupp would benefit from Paul's death and become the Director of Theater if the position was funded, giving him a motive. Ben had mentioned a music professor that Quinn would have to talk to, and she needed to speak with Lenny Mishler as soon as he was well enough. Mishler might be willing to talk about what he saw in the Green Room that motivated him to preach to Paul.

She checked her phone for a message from Ed, but no luck. She hoped he wasn't tied up in court. The lounge was warm and stuffy, and she was getting sleepy. She stretched her legs and again thought about what she'd found in Ben's kitchen.

Was he a murder-for-hire guy, a financial swindler, or wanted by Interpol? She had better keep a poker face around him until she found out.

Chapter 10

Quinn stood at the window, watching the gusty winds pile fresh snow on the just-plowed campus sidewalks. A lone man slogged through the storm, holding an umbrella. Just as he neared the building, the wind swooped his umbrella up Mary Poppins style, dousing him with snow. As Dr. Jerry Knupp yanked the door open, a crack of thunder had him nearly jumping out of his skin.

"Dr. Knupp?" Quinn asked as a whoosh of cold air blasted her.

He was in his late forties, a decade older than his photograph. He'd lost weight since the picture was made, and his face was all angles and sharp cheekbones. His ginger hair was now long and gray, accentuating his narrow face.

"Yes," he said, squinting at her.

She introduced herself and explained she wanted to talk about Dr. Loughty.

He didn't look happy as Quinn steered him toward the lounge. "Let's talk in here. I won't take much of your time."

Jerry Knupp settled himself in a chair, balanced his briefcase on his knees, and looked at her expectantly. "I've told the police everything I know," he said. "Have you spoken with Dr. Beckett? He's the head of the department, and I think you should speak to him first."

"I've talked with both Dr. Beckett and Ms. Featherston. She was kind enough to tell me you were returning from class. I'm an investigator for the Meadows law firm, representing Dr. Loughty's estate, and I just have a few questions." Before Knupp could comment, Quinn asked, "How long were you and Dr. Loughty colleagues?"

"No one was *collegial* with Paul," he said, putting the briefcase on the floor, looking as ready to talk as Sally had been. "We worked around each other. He was a user. He wrung the rest of us dry of whatever he wanted, then tossed us aside. Working with him was a living hell."

"Then why did you stay at the college?"

"I have tenure. That means the College can't get rid of me easily. I would have to commit a gross act to be fired, and at my age, I wasn't going to walk away from a tenured position. I had no choice but to endure what Paul dished out. I didn't kill him, but I won't say I'll miss him. You look shocked by what I said because you've been talking to Sally. She was over the moon about Paul. Couldn't quit singing his praises."

"Was something going on between them?"

"Of course not." He shrugged one shoulder and cocked his head to the side. "Paul liked his women a whole lot younger than Sally. He sweet-talked her so she would do the extra work he wanted her to do for him. Paul was talented, maybe even gifted, but he was a liar and an embarrassment to the rest of us. He schmoozed the wealthy Alderberry widow for a year after her husband died, telling the poor woman that thousands of students would walk through the theater doors and remember her husband. Horseshit. Marvin Alderberry was a small-time tinkerer who created a useful doodad for the manufacturing industry. She was elderly and lonely, and Paul took advantage of her. He was still twisting her arm to give more and even asked her to endow a scholarship in her husband's name."

Jerry Knupp seemed keen to speak ill of a murdered man whose job he might get, and he had the overly eager look of someone ready to dish dirt. "Paul was morally corrupt. My God, he swung both ways. He did whatever made him feel good with whoever was at hand. He wasn't picky as long as they were nubile and young. We lost an up-and-coming male theater student to the English department because of Paul. Tiberius would never have sued the college if Paul hadn't screwed him, then ditched him. But our Paul wasn't alone for long. He hooked up with a girl right away."

Knupp's outrage amused Quinn. If Ben were right about Jerry Knupp, he'd had an affair with Roxie while married to Rhea. Maybe there were more hedonists than just Paul in the department.

Knupp jabbed a bony finger at Quinn. "Paul called his new girlfriend his Italian Hottie." His eyes narrowed. "You are aware of Margarite, aren't you?"

"Yes, I knew they spent some time together. I didn't know about the nickname." Quinn felt her phone vibrate in her messenger bag and hoped it was Ed Adams, leaving a message that he'd be available later.

"Margarite is hot as a pistol on stage. When I first met her, I thought she was a mousy little thing that needed a fine arts elective course because she wasn't actress material. Then I posted tryouts for *Streetcar Named Desire* and saw she had signed up to read for the part of Blanche. I hoped I could let her down easily. But she walked on stage and became Blanche DuBois. She made you believe she was the sexiest woman on earth. The heat on the stage was incredible, so the other actors, particularly the one who played Stella, upped their game. It was the best production of *Streetcar* I've ever directed, and shortly after our run ended, Paul was screwing Margarite."

Quinn thought Knupp must be tone-deaf, or he was so narcissistic he believed no one would tell her about his affair with Roxie.

"Margarite was the last in a long line of students Paul abused," Knupp said. "Poor girl thought Paul would marry her."

"Did Dr. Beckett know about Dr. Loughty's behavior with students?"

"Of course, he did. He turned a blind eye to all of Paul's shenanigans because the money he raised made Beckett look good to the dean. Beckett wants to be promoted to provost and needs the dean in his pocket. Of course, once the press finds out what's happened on Beckett's watch, he'll be lucky to keep his current job. It wasn't only Paul's horn-dogging that was the issue for the rest of us. You should talk to Dale Wilkerson in the Music Department. He's the most talented young professor we've had in years, and Paul denied him tenure. That's academic-speak for you're fired. He's in his office right now, packing."

"Why did Dr. Loughty deny him tenure?"

"I'll let Dale tell you. It's his story."

"All right. I'll go around and see him." If Knupp was telling the truth, Dale Wilkerson had a motive for murder. "Sally told me Roxie Ryland was Dr. Loughty's assistant this term. Were there any difficulties between them?"

"You'll have to ask Roxie. I'm her thesis adviser, and I think she is an asset to the program. Roxie was Paul's assistant director on his current show and was at the rehearsal with him on Sunday evening. I guess that makes her and the crew the last people to see Paul alive." He scribbled Roxie's cell phone number on a chit of paper and handed it to Quinn. "She has an office on the third floor of the library with the rest of the graduate assistants."

A stream of noisy students passed the lounge and pushed out into the storm, letting a gust of cold air in. One of them called out to Knupp, and he raised his hand and gave an awkward wave.

Knupp had become restless, and Quinn pressed her advantage. "Dr. Beckett said you would assume Dr. Loughty's position as Director of Theater. Are you looking forward to the new job?"

"Of course I am. It doesn't mean I killed Paul. I'm the best person to take charge of the program, and I'll hire my replacement. The new hire and I will turn this department around."

"Do you have anyone in mind?"

"We have a very competent student finishing our graduate program."

"Roxie Ryland?"

Knupp went stiff. "Roxie graduates this term and is welcome to apply." Knupp stood and picked up his briefcase. "I have office hours beginning in ten minutes."

"Did you know Paul was using cocaine?"

Knupp gave her a condescending look. "Of course not. You're wrong if you think he was murdered over drugs. Someone killed him because he was a first-class jerk. You have no idea what's been happening here," he said too loudly.

"One more thing. Where were you on Sunday night?"

"In my office, grading papers. It was Rhea's Bunko night, and I couldn't think straight with a hen party going on. I went to my office to work. Roxie dropped by after rehearsal and left the revisions on her thesis for me to review. Good day." With that, he left and lumbered down the hall.

Quinn pulled out her phone and called Ed Adams. She was relieved to hear his voice when he said, "Hi, Quinn. Nice to hear from you."

"I'm in trouble," Quinn told him.

"Sorry to hear that. What's happening?"

"My home loan was sold, and the new owner will foreclose if I don't pay the balance in thirty days. I don't have the money."

"I assume your bank notified you who the purchaser is?"

"Yes, Grand Summit Bank. Can you do anything about the foreclosure?"

"They have to file a foreclosure notice. They can't just turn up on your porch and demand you get out. I'll call the bank and let them know I represent you, but I think the bank will do this by the book. They won't bring the bank regulators down on their necks. No one wants the scrutiny of the feds. The bank may eventually get the house, but I can slow it down, so you have some breathing space to get moved."

Adams told her the foreclosure would go by the book, though Truck didn't believe it would. A lot depended upon which one of them was correct. "Have

you considered filing a complaint on your original bank with the Federal Reserve?" he asked. "It's odd for a bank to sell a single loan to a private bank."

"Can you do that for me?"

"All right, sure."

"I have another problem. Detective Deke Bystrom has lodged a complaint with the state licensing board, claiming I passed myself off as cop to a woman I interviewed."

"Have you received a formal notice from the board?"

"Not yet."

"Did you record the interview with the woman?" he asked.

"No, and I didn't see her record it. I identified myself as an investigator with Meadows Law Firm. Several times in fact."

"If there is no recording, it's your word against hers. Who is she?"

"Margarite Mancini, a college student who was having an affair with Paul Loughty, a client of ours who was murdered. His brother hired the firm to represent him, and Bystrom is the investigating officer."

"I see. It's odd that Margarite didn't make the accusation directly to the board. Usually, the person with the beef files the complaint, but there's bad blood between you and Bystrom. I don't see this complaint going anywhere if neither of you recorded the interview. Cheer up. You may never have to work with Bystrom again depending on how Judge Hartley rules in the D.P.D. case."

"I don't want my license to depend on how Judge Hartley rules on the case."

"I can handle this, so you aren't dependent on the case ruling. Let me know if you get a formal notice from the board. Call me, and we'll work together to answer their questions, but I think the board will table the complaint before it gets that far." Ed closed the call with a promise to stay in touch. She felt better knowing she had an advocate.

While she hiked across campus to interview Dr. Wilkerson, she checked her email for a copy of the college surveillance video from Sunday night. She hadn't received it and hoped it was only an oversight of the campus police, not the result of Bystrom's meddling. She left a message for Meadows and asked him to make a second request for the video.

Quinn pulled her coat tighter against the cold lash of the wind. She wouldn't put it past Jerry Knupp to be on the phone with Roxie, telling her that an investigator was heading her way. Maybe Roxie killed Paul for a job working for her lover. She was among the last to see Paul alive.

Chapter 11

Quinn found the soon-to-be-gone music professor's office tucked away at the end of a hall near the restrooms. His office was slightly larger than a good-sized closet, and the desk and floor were a jumble of boxes and files. Dale Wilkerson was close to her age, in his late twenties, and probably dreading the advent of the big three-oh. He had a stubble beard, spiky, gel-mussed dark hair, jeans, and a band T-shirt washed so often she couldn't read the print. He was tall and slender, with long fingers that could probably reach over an octave on a piano. Perfect for his profession.

He was holding a roll of packing tape when he looked up at Quinn. "Hi, can I help you?"

"I'm Quinn Kane. I work for the law firm representing Paul Loughty's estate. Got a few minutes?"

"Okay, why not? The cops have already quizzed me. I'd say have a seat, but there's no place. Want a beer?" He pointed to a dorm-size refrigerator tucked under his desk.

"No, thanks." Drinking in his office was a no-no, but what was the worst that could happen? The guy was already fired. "Are you moving to a new job?"

He knocked back the rest of his beer. "Hell no. Thanks to Paul Loughty, I'll be lucky to get a janitor's job in a community theater. I earned a doctorate in musical theater and worked my fingers to the bone for years, only to have him fire me."

"One person can do that?"

"Oh, yes, and enjoy himself while he's sticking it to you. Paul was the chairperson of my tenure committee. I came here on a tenure track position, meaning if I slaved away and kissed everyone's ass for six years, I had a shot at tenure. Once you get it, it's almost impossible for them to get rid of you. So, they ax you after using you for six years, then get another poor bastard who just got out of school and use him for the next six years. Saves on salaries to hire the young'uns."

He crushed the beer can and tossed it into the trash. "I never saw it coming. Paul did a performance review with me every year and never said a negative word about my work. When the tenure committee denied me, Paul didn't even have the decency to tell me. After I ordered textbooks for my spring classes, the bookstore manager called and told me I wasn't on the faculty for the spring semester. I was floored. I hunted down Paul and asked him what was going on, and you know what he said? He told me he couldn't talk about the tenure process."

"How did you feel about that?"

"I lost it. I was yelling like crazy, and Paul was grinning from ear to ear. He thought it was so damn funny that I had to find out from the bookstore that I was fired. One thing I know, if Paul Loughty had voted for me, not one of those milquetoast losers on the committee would have voted against me."

"I'm sorry."

"Really?" He slammed a book down. "People always say they're sorry. Do you have a doctorate and all the debt I piled up getting through school? Have you ever been fired?"

"I don't have a doctorate and haven't been fired, but I have student debt, and I've worked hard to be where I am."

He stopped packing and ran his hand through his hair. "Sorry, I was out of line." He pulled another beer out of the refrigerator and popped the top. "Sure you won't have one?"

Again, she shook her head.

"Look, I have nothing good to say about Paul, but I didn't kill him. Someone else got the pleasure of doing that, and I have an alibi. On Sunday night, I was playing my sax at Peaches D-Lite, my favorite drag queen bar on Federal Boulevard. You can call and check. At least I still have a part-time gig blowing my horn."

"Who do you think killed Paul?"

Wilkerson slammed an empty file drawer shut, then yanked open another and grabbed some folders. "Anyone. I bet it was one of his long string of jilted lovers." He tossed a stack of sheet music into a box, turned, and looked at her. "Dr. Knupp is getting Paul's job. Isn't that what you investigator types call a motive for murder?"

Before Quinn could answer, a tall, rangy young man knocked on Wilkerson's door. "I'm sorry to interrupt. I need a moment."

"Come in," Wilkerson said. He glanced at Quinn and said, "This is Tiberius Clarke-Watson." To the young man, he said, "This is Quinn Kane. An investigator looking into Paul's murder."

"I understand you were a student of Dr. Loughty's," Quinn said.

Tiberius swallowed, his big Adam's Apple bobbing up and down.

"Go ahead, Tiberius," Wilkerson said. "It's okay to talk truth to crazy. Tell her why you got the hell out of the drama department."

Tiberius picked an invisible piece of lint from his sweater and swallowed again. "I don't know about talking about Paul now that he's dead."

Wilkerson put his arm around Tiberius' shoulders and hugged him. "It's okay. She ought to hear it."

Tiberius kept his eyes downcast. "I couldn't take it anymore."

"I'm sorry," Quinn said," I don't understand."

"He got screwed like the rest of us by Paul," Wilkerson said.

Tiberius wiped his eyes on the sleeves of his sweater. "I shouldn't have gotten involved with him. I knew his reputation, but I fell in love with him. When he broke it off with me, he turned mean. I think he was embarrassed that he had taken a Black gay lover. I still love him. It hurt so bad to see him with Margarite, and she was such a bitch, telling me Paul was going to marry her." He wiped his eyes and thrust a handful of papers toward Wilkerson. "I came by to give you this. I didn't turn it in after the last show."

Wilkerson dropped the papers in a box. "You did the right thing by switching majors. Come by the club tonight and have a drink with me."

Tiberius nodded and edged out the door. "I have to get upstairs to work."

Wilkerson turned to Quinn with a glint in his eye. "You didn't know Paul took men to his bed?"

Quinn shook her head. "It doesn't matter to me unless it has something to do with his death."

A sly smile crossed his face. "Tiberius and I were

lovers, too. I'm not timid about enjoying the pleasures of the flesh. Even that dried-up old fart Beckett was getting some. Girls only, and probably in the missionary position, but the old guy was in the game. Paul and Jerry Knupp were swapping out with Foxie Roxie. What a farce this place is. I bet you didn't know that Roxie was arrested in Knupp's front yard for trespassing and disturbing the peace. She and Knupp's wife got into a hair-pulling fight over their man. You wouldn't think anyone would fight over old Knupp, would you? Now, he gets Paul's job and the girl, and I got the boot. Sweet, no?"

"How do you think Margarite would have reacted if Paul told her he wouldn't marry her?"

"Did he tell her that?"

"Just a hypothetical question."

"Margarite is about as deep as a birdbath, but I can't see her shooting him." Wilkerson ground his beer can under his foot and left it on the floor.

"Where does Tiberius work?" Quinn asked.

"English department, top of the stairs. Hey," Wilkerson added, "Tiberius was at the club Sunday night and came home with me. He spent the night."

Quinn left Wilkerson taping his boxes shut. Both he and Tiberius had a reason to kill Paul. While she climbed the stairs to the English department, she called the manager of Peaches D-Lite. He wasn't there, but the assistant manager who had worked the night Paul was killed verified Wilkerson had played with the band until the club closed at two a.m. When she asked him if Wilkerson had left alone, the manager said a young black man had been with him. Quinn hung up, thinking Peaches D-Lite was within walking distance of the college. Bands took breaks. Neither Wilkerson's nor Tiberius's alibis were airtight.

Wilkerson had been keen to describe the debauchery, even claiming Dr. Beckett was involved. There were more hedonists than Paul in the department. She wondered if any of the other professors had demanded sex in return for a leg up to the professional stage.

They all had access to the theater, were familiar with Paul's schedule, and their fingerprints would be in the Green Room. Plenty of them had a reason to want Paul dead. Which one gained the most?

Quinn found Tiberius sitting in a workroom, stapling papers together. He didn't look happy to see her. In the music professor's office, he'd seemed genuinely grieving Paul's death, but he was an actor. Like Margarite, he could be mourning that he killed his lover.

She remained standing by Tiberius, forcing him to look up at her. "Why did you drop the lawsuit against Dr. Loughty and the College?"

"How do you know about that?"

"It's my job."

He folded his hands in his lap. "I should have never filed it. It was a stupid idea."

She waited until the silence bothered him enough he talked.

"When I hired the lawyer, I was mad and hurt. He egged me on to file the suit. Something about getting a landmark decision, and he said the college would settle instead of going to court." He wiped the tears from his eyes. "I think he just wanted a chance to get a chunk of money." Tiberius wiped his face on his sweater.

"Who do you think killed Paul?"

He shook his head.

"What do you think Margarite would do if Paul told her he wouldn't marry her?"

"Did he tell her that?" Tiberius asked hopefully.

"I don't know." Quinn shrugged.

"She's a manipulative airhead, but she loved him. I don't think she had it in her to kill him."

Contrary to Tiberius's belief, a manipulative airhead whose man might be looking back at Roxie could commit murder.

"Where were you on Sunday evening?"

He looked uncomfortable. Quinn stared at him until he answered. "At Peaches D-Lite on Federal."

She wondered if Wilkerson had time to phone and prep him. "Did you see or talk to anyone?"

"Dale Wilkerson was playing that night. I went home with him."

"Did Paul ever promise you he could find you a job?"

Tiberius looked away.

Quinn put her card on the table. "Call me if you think of anything else."

She took the elevator to the library's top floor, thinking Paul was loved, hated, or admired, but no one liked him.

Half the library's top floor was closed storage; the rest was a large open space filled with partitioned cubicles. Quinn was glad she'd told Roxie that she was coming. Finding her in the rabbit warren of noisy cubicles would have been like finding her way out of a maze.

A statuesque brunette walked toward her. "Ms. Kane? I'm Roxie Ryland."

"Yes, I'm Quinn. Thank you for meeting me."

"I'm back this way." Roxie weaved through a maze of cubicles.

Quinn heard the low murmur of voices, the occasional curse, and the whir of a printer. It would be hard to concentrate here and write a thesis.

Roxie stopped in front of a cubicle decorated with theater posters.

Quinn squeezed in behind her and took a seat. "Dr. Knupp told me you were at the rehearsal Sunday."

Roxie nodded. "I was there. I'm Paul's graduate assistant this term. He'd called a tech rehearsal for the sound crew and wanted me to help train them. Melinda Garcia and Todd Evans are freshmen and unfamiliar with the computer programs. The four of us were there Sunday night."

"Were you there for the entire rehearsal?"

"All four of us were together from four-thirty until about six-thirty. Paul had pizza and drinks delivered, and we ate in the Green Room after rehearsal. Paul made some script changes, and we took notes, but all of us were anxious to leave. A storm was blowing in and was supposed to dump up to a foot of new snow. But Paul kept us, making more changes to the script. He finally let Todd and Melinda go but kept me back. He wanted to discuss whether we should replace Melinda or give her time to catch on. I told him I would work with her this week, and we agreed to talk again at the end of the week. He and I walked out together, and Paul told me he was going to pick up a sandwich and go back and work."

"But he had pizza delivered." Quinn knew from the autopsy report that Paul hadn't eaten pizza.

"Paul didn't eat unhealthy food. The last time I saw

him, he was walking toward the bagel place on campus."

There was a curse from the next workspace.

"Someone's research isn't going well," Roxie said.

"Sounds like it. Did you go straight home from rehearsal?"

Roxie shook her head. "I dropped by Dr. Knupp's office to ask him some questions about my thesis. We talked for a moment, but I was in a hurry to get home. The weather was bad, and I was tired. I caught the light rail from the campus station on Colfax and went home."

Once again, Quinn had one suspect provide an alibi for another. But both suspects were on campus Sunday night when Paul was murdered. Either Knupp or Roxie could have killed him.

"Do you remember if Paul locked the theater when you two left?"

"Yes, he did. Probably everyone has already told you he was obsessed with keeping the doors locked."

"What did the Green Room look like Sunday afternoon?"

Roxie smiled. "Like it always does, messy. It always needs scrubbing. The light-colored floor shows everything."

Quinn pressed Roxie on the fine details. "Was there anything unusual on the floor, a spilled soft drink maybe?"

Roxie frowned. "I don't remember. Wait. I took a picture of Melinda and Todd. They were sitting on the floor eating pizza and goofing around." She scrolled through her phone and held it out to Quinn.

Quinn zoomed in for a closer look. It was a wide shot, including the floor from the sofa to the door. The photo was time-dated shortly after six in the evening, and there were no blood stains on the floor. "Would you send that to me?"

"Sure." Roxie forwarded the picture to Quinn's email.

"Did Paul seem upset Sunday?"

"No, he was in one of his excited moods. He was always like that at the beginning of a show."

"What was he like?"

Roxie's face softened. "He was the smartest man I ever met and so creative. Both are difficult personality traits for his colleagues or a partner. I was his graduate assistant and, at one time, his partner. It was hard to be with Paul. He drove himself relentlessly. He was terrified of being forgotten or becoming irrelevant. When he was writing or directing a play, if it wasn't going well, he was depressed and anxious, had trouble sleeping, and wanted to be left alone. But if his work was going great, he wanted to party and have a crowd around him. Paul used people to keep his energy level high. Before you ask, I ended our relationship. It was too hard being with a sybarite. He lived for pleasure, and he didn't follow conventional rules. I'd never met anyone like him, and for a while, I thought he was the most attractive man in the world. Most of the time, it was sublime, but I couldn't take his dark periods."

"Do you still love him?"

Her mouth curled into a smile. "No, it would be so romantic to say that a part of me will always love Paul, but it isn't true. Living with him was exhausting, and one morning, I woke up and felt nothing. That's when I left him. I wasn't jealous of Margarite. Paul and I had an affair, nothing more. Both of us knew it wasn't going to last forever. We had a bit of fun. That's all."

Chapter 12

On her way back to Sally Featherston's office, Quinn stopped in front of the Alderberry Theater to look closely at the memorial the widow had funded to keep her husband's name alive. The building sat on the boundary line of the campus. Twin sidewalks ran along the sides and led to the stage door at the back. A parking lot was on the west side of the theater, the drama department was to the east, and behind the theater was city land and a copse of dense woods.

Like the rest of the campus, the theater was built of red brick. But the similarity ended there. It was an aggressively modern concoction of sharp angles, corner windows, and large expanses of glass. Marvin Alderberry's name was inscribed on a lintel over the impressive double front doors. Quinn checked the front of the theater for security cameras. One was attached to a light pole and aimed at the front door. She studied the area, the eaves, and even the trees lining the walkway and found no other surveillance. It was an oversight on someone's part. Quinn was sure someone at the college was combing the budget to find the money to beef up security on campus.

Quinn wanted to catch Sally Featherston while she was rushing to leave and beat the storm. She would be less apt to push back when Quinn asked her for a key to the theater.

Sally was just getting off the phone when Quinn walked in and asked to borrow a key. "Whatever for? Detective Bystrom told me I shouldn't let anyone in there. There's still crime scene tape up. Nope, I can't do it."

Quinn appealed to the woman's need to feel she was helping find Paul's killer. "I can't do a decent job for Dr. Loughty unless I see where he died. The crime scene techs have already gotten everything they need, and I promise I won't touch anything."

"This better be okay." Sally picked through a desk drawer full of keys, read the paper disks, and tossed them back until she found the right one. Looking over her shoulder at Dr. Beckett's closed office door, she hesitated before pressing a key in Quinn's outstretched hand. "My door stays open for students to use the workroom. If I'm not here when you come back, don't give the key to anyone, and don't let anyone see you put it back right here." She jabbed her finger at the center desk drawer. "I could lose my job over this. And don't forget to lock the theater. It's going to be near zero tonight, and the homeless will get in there and make a mess. One other thing. Don't turn the light out over the stage door. We keep it on all the time."

"Thanks. You've been a big help. Will Dr. Beckett be much longer?"

Before Sally could answer, an angry student burst out of Beckett's office and stalked past Sally and Quinn. Beckett stood behind his desk, shaking his head.

"Dr. Beckett," Quinn said as she walked into his office and closed the door behind her.

"I was just about to leave. I have a meeting."

"This won't take long."

Beckett looked displeased. He remained standing, and she did, too.

"It seems that sexual relationships between faculty and students were common in this department."

His nostrils flared, and his eyes flashed with anger. "How dare you come in here and make accusations."

"I'm not accusing anyone of anything. I'm telling you what I was told."

An angry red flush crept up his neck. "You've been hoodwinked into believing gossip. We are a team of talented people who work closely together. Absolutely nothing like what you're insinuating ever happened."

She carefully placed her business card on his desk. "The sexual exploits between faculty and students will come to light during the murder investigation. It would be advantageous for you to have already acknowledged there is a problem. Call me if you'd like to tell your side of the story."

Quinn left him standing, staring after her. She thought she'd played fair with Dr. Beckett. She'd allowed him time to give his superior a heads up and time to lawyer up. No one wanted to be caught with their pants down when a sex scandal went public.

The sky had grown darker while she had talked with Sally and Beckett. The winter sun sat balanced on the mountaintops, and soon, it would tumble down the backside and plunge Denver into another bitterly cold evening. As she turned on the sidewalk to the back of the theater, two bone-thin homeless men with hollowed-out faces walked out of the woods and passed her. They were a stark contrast to the student hurrying along, holding a five-dollar cup of coffee and staring at her phone.

Dr. Beckett had dismissed the homeless as a

pestilence and blamed them for Paul's murder, which was stereotypical and unfair. The homeless might be guilty of petty theft or mugging, but murder was a reach. Besides, Paul was killed by someone he knew, and the killer was so enraged he didn't notice Paul was dead after the first bullet.

She rounded the corner and saw a light burning over the stage door. A low stone wall separated the school's property from the tract of undeveloped woods where the homeless camped. The city council had passed a controversial no-camping ban before realizing that the city didn't have the resources to house the needy. The council designated the woods behind the college as a temporary homeless camp over a howl of protests from the college and the downtown business owners, but the woods wouldn't remain raw land for long. Developers were drooling over plans to turn it into a forest of luxury high-rise buildings.

She stood by the wall and noticed two snow-packed paths led into the woods. One veered off in the direction of Colfax Avenue. Though she could hear the street traffic, the trees were too dense for her to see the cars whizzing by. The second trail was more well-traveled and meandered deeper into the trees. With no surveillance on the back of the theater, the killer could have used either route to the stage door and never been caught on video. The surveillance video from the front camera aimed at the front door wouldn't tell the whole story of who was at the theater on Sunday night, a significant complication to her finding Paul's killer.

Quinn plucked the sagging yellow crime scene tape off the stage door. It was solid and had a sturdy lock. It wouldn't have been easy to pick the lock, and there was no sign it had been kicked in. The door was either unlocked Sunday night, the killer had a key, or an accomplice let the killer in. She hoped Sally had a list of people she had given keys to.

Quinn went inside and locked the door behind her. The air smelled cloyingly stale and was cold enough to raise goosebumps on her arms. A long hallway divided the front of the house from the backstage areas. Twin security lights cast shallow pools of yellow light on the floor. To her left were thick black curtains that hid the actor's entrance from the stage. From her high school days as a stagehand, she knew an identical actor's access would be at the far end of the hall.

She poked her head into the first door and found Lenny Mishler's scene shop. She flipped on the overhead lights. Tool hung on the walls by size and type, and a sheet of plywood leaned against a table saw. Receipts, set drawings, and scribbled notes covered the top of a metal desk. There wasn't a speck of sawdust in sight, and the trash bins were empty.

As she turned off the lights and stepped into the hall, the storm struck with sudden fury. Ice pellets hammered on the roof, the wind rattled through the attic, and the building complained with ghostly creaks and moans. It was the perfect soundtrack for an ambush, though she doubted Latham's men were lurking inside.

The Green Room was next door to the scene shop. It was small and furnished with a sofa, a round coffee table, two chairs, and a narrow table snug against the back wall. The room was a pigsty. Pizza boxes with pieces of dried crust, fast-food sacks, dirty ashtrays on every flat surface, and cigarette butts floating in half-filled coffee cups. Loose papers covered every flat surface. Fingerprint powder coated everything. The room held hundreds of fingerprints and enough DNA to keep a lab busy for weeks.

The walls were nicked and smudged, and someone had kicked a hole in the sheetrock above a baseboard. The only fresh paint was high in one corner, a lighter shade than the rest of the room. It looked like someone had patched a hole, but why would they repair the smaller hole and leave the gaping one?

Quinn stood near where Paul died and visualized how the murder might have happened. He sat on the sofa, eating a sandwich with his booze on the table. It was only ten feet from where he sat to the door. When his killer walked in, Paul felt safe enough to let the person walk up to him. He trusted his visitor enough to stay seated. Maybe the gun was hidden behind the killer's back or in a pocket. Perhaps they talked before Paul was shot and slumped over on his side. It should have been evident to the killer that the professor was dead. Yet, the murderer stepped closer and shot him again.

A purple stain on the sofa caught Quinn's attention. It was the distinct shade of purple that acid phosphate turned when it touched semen. If the police included this lab result in their public statement, it would be a juicy tidbit for the press, and the sex scandal would blow sky-high. Dr. Beckett should be covering his backside now rather than later.

Something about the crime scene nagged at Quinn. She turned her attention to the evidence markers, little numbered tents, marking the blood trail between the threshold and the sofa. Some drops were no bigger than a speck and none larger than a quarter. They weren't evenly spaced. A few were clustered together; others were random distances apart. She looked out in the beige-tiled hallway. There wasn't a speck of blood on the hall tiles, and it was unlikely that the hall floor had been cleaned after midnight Sunday and before eight Monday morning when Lenny Mishler found the body. The police would have noticed if Lenny had been bleeding. If it wasn't the shop foreman's blood, whose was it? Had someone been here after Paul was killed and before Mishler arrived?

Her instincts were humming as she took pictures. The blood trail made no sense to her. She didn't believe the killer cleaned the hall and left his blood on the floor. The drops weren't smudged like the killer walked through the trail when he arrived or left. The killer had been close enough to watch Paul die, organized enough to take the gun, yet left his blood at the scene. It didn't add up.

Quinn needed Doc Iverson's expert opinion, and she knew he didn't like interruptions. When he answered her call, he sounded gruff and distracted. "I gave you my notes from the autopsy report. What do you want now?"

"I need your expert opinion about the blood trail on the floor at the Loughty crime scene."

"Don't butter me up. I hate that expert shit. I've seen the photos, even went over there, and took a look once I got that dingbat secretary to let me in. I'll call you when I have something, and it won't be today."

Doc was cantankerous and had the social skills of a rattlesnake, but he was brilliant and true to his word. She'd have to be patient. Her least favorite activity.

Before she left the Green Room, she called the college's main number and worked her way through the phone tree to the facilities maintenance department. She identified herself as an investigator in the Loughty murder case and asked when the Green Room was last cleaned.

The guy who answered must have thought she was connected with the police, and she didn't correct him. He told her a crew had cleaned late Friday afternoon, and the door was locked at five o'clock when the cleaners left. She asked about the fresh patch and new paint in the top corner of the room. He explained they'd cut into the sheetrock to fix an electrical problem. She glanced up in the corner where the patch was and down to the baseboard. There were no electrical plugs on the wall. Something about the patch still bothered her.

Still, she hung up, satisfied her hunch was correct. The blood trail was made after rehearsal and before eight on Monday morning. She turned off the lights in the Green Room and went to the men's dressing room. The sinks and mirrors were spotless, and the floor was so clean that it smelled of disinfectant.

The women's dressing room was on the other side of a sizeable janitor's closet. Before she could flip the light switch, something brushed her hair as it swept past her in the dark. Then, the air around her came alive. Creatures whooshed; something soft grazed her arm.

Waving her arms above her head like a madwoman, Quinn found the light switch and snapped it on. A row of gray bats hung on the pipe grid in the ceiling, taking flight like planes on a flight line, sweeping around her and out the door.

She willed herself to stay still and allow the swarm to find her position and fly around her. When the thrumming of the wings stilled, she saw that the women's dressing room was clean and orderly except for the fresh bat guano on the floor.

She returned to the hall and saw the stage curtains swaying. The heating system blew them, or someone passed through them while the bats diverted her attention. The stage door had been locked, and she had bolted it behind her, but it didn't mean she was alone.

Quinn slipped into the voluminous drapes. A single security light lit the empty stage before her. To her left was a spiral staircase. Another security light glowed at the bottom. She knew the stairs led to the trap room from her days crewing for shows. She'd worked the traps, pulling the doors open on the stage floor to let actors enter or exit the stage dramatically.

Suddenly, thunder cracked so loudly that she felt the wall tremble beneath her hand. As the rumbling faded, she heard the soft scuff of a shoe and felt that awful sensation of being watched.

Even the building seemed to be holding its breath.

There, a scrape. Then, a rustle. Somewhere in the dark, someone was moving. Fear skittered down her spine. Inside the heavy drapes, she couldn't discern whether it came from behind her or below her in the trap room.

Suddenly, the air was heavy with a malevolent presence.

Now, a rush of air from behind her. Then a hard shove and Quinn tumbled down the stairs, whacking her head on the first curve, picking up speed as she rolled pell-mell, spiraling toward the bottom. Her left shoulder crashed into the unforgiving steel when she rounded the second turn. Sharp pain took her breath away, but she grabbed a rail, righted herself on the bottom step, and waited until her eyes grew accustomed to the dim light in the trap room.

Creak, shuffle.

Someone was hurrying across the wood-floored stage above her head. She stood and scanned the ceiling, tracking the footsteps moving above her.

With a few more steps, the person would be over the trap door in the center of the stage.

A shuffled step above her, then another. Quinn held her breath, waiting in place under the trap door.

Now! She yanked on the steel drawbar, dropping the trap door with a bang.

Chapter 13

A screaming figure landed in a heap on a stack of old blankets at Quinn's feet. Just as Quinn approached to help, the heavily clothed figure jumped up, and tiny fists punched the air around her head. A blow glanced off Quinn's cheek with no more heft than a bat's wing. Quinn wrangled a hold on the flailing arms and held them with one hand while she jerked the hoodie off.

The cadaverous old woman shook like a leaf. Wispy gray hair stuck out from her pink scalp, and startling blue eyes stared straight into Quinn's. "Let go of me. I haven't done anything wrong."

"You pushed me down a flight of stairs." Quinn dropped her grip on the woman and took a step back. The woman was under five feet tall and probably tipped the scales at ninety pounds.

The woman rubbed her wrists. "Are you a cop?"

"I'm an investigator." Quinn pulled out her ID and held it up.

The woman leaned close and squinted at the card.

"Are you hurt?" Quinn asked.

She looked at Quinn warily. "I've been better."

"Maybe you should sit on the steps over there and make sure you're okay." Quinn moved aside, leaving plenty of room for her to pass without feeling threatened.

The woman's knees popped when she squatted. She pulled up her pant legs and pressed her fingertips to a bruise. "My knee hurts." She gingerly bent and extended the knee. "Nothing's broken." She looked up at Quinn. "You scared me bad. I wasn't doing anything in here but getting out of the storm. My bones hurt bad in this cold." She shook her finger at Quinn. "Can't an old woman get no peace? I never stole anything, and I don't bother anyone."

"What's your name?"

"Alice Whitlock." She chuckled. "Those bats are something, aren't they?"

"Do you sleep in here often?"

Alice pulled herself up straighter and tried to look fierce. "Never said I slept in here."

"A man was killed here," Quinn said gently. "His name was Paul Loughty. Did you know him?"

"Never heard of him. Where's that other detective who was around here?"

"At the station. When did you see him?"

Alice tucked her head. "Monday morning. I was watching from the woods. He saw me and came over and asked a bunch of questions. I told him I didn't know anything about the dead guy. He got mean and told me if he saw me again, he'd run me in for vagrancy. It shouldn't be a crime to be homeless."

Quinn nodded. "There are a couple of us working the case. Do you remember his name?"

Alice shook her head.

But when Quinn asked Alice to describe the detective, Alice gave a good description of Deke Bystrom.

"Did you sleep in here Sunday night?"

Alice crossed her arms over her chest and stared at the ground.

"I work for a law firm. I'm not a cop. I won't share what you tell me with Detective Bystrom."

Alice shook her head. "I shouldn't have come back Monday morning. I just wanted to make sure someone found that poor man. I don't want nothing to do with the cops."

"What time were you here Sunday night?"

"I got here after ten-thirty. I don't ever come in earlier because they work in here all hours of the day and even on the weekends. Hope House closes at ten-thirty, and I was too late to get a bed. I sure was sorry. They serve a good breakfast. But I came straight over here."

"Where do you sleep?"

"In the janitor's closet. That's where I was when you woke up the bats. It's over by the men's bathroom."

"Do you walk across the stage or use the hallway to get to the closet?"

"I walk across the stage. I don't want to run into any students. Sometimes, they're in that little room that looks like a living room. I like to keep to myself."

Paul was already dead when Alice crossed the stage. "Did you hear anything?"

Alice shook her head. "Slept like a baby."

Quinn sensed that Alice wasn't revealing everything she knew but wasn't surprised. Information was the coin of the realm on the streets. "Something woke you up, didn't it?"

Alice chewed her bottom lip before speaking so softly that Quinn had to lean forward to hear her. "A man woke me up with his hollering. I opened the door and saw him clear as a day, running out of that living room to the back door."

"Did he see you?"

"No." She shivered. "I closed the door and stayed in the closet for a long time. Then I went and peeked in there, and I wish I hadn't seen that dead man. It was terrible."

"What time did the man wake you?"

She shoved up her sleeve and showed Quinn a man's Timex watch strapped to her thin arm. "I got me a watch. I saw him right after eleven o'clock."

"Would you recognize him?"

"What if he comes after me?" Alice shuddered.

"I can keep you safe."

"Why should I trust you?"

"You already trust me, or you wouldn't have told me what happened." Quinn pulled out her phone and showed her Ben's picture and a picture of her last boyfriend, which she should have deleted long before. "Have you ever seen either of these men?"

Alice tapped her gnarled finger on the picture of Ben. "That's him. He was the one screaming."

Quinn worked hard to hide her reaction. "Are you sure, Alice?"

"Course, I'm sure. I'm old. I'm not blind or stupid."

"I didn't mean to suggest you were." Quinn's chest was tight, and her stomach was churning. It was a good news-bad news kind of deal. Alice provided Ben with an alibi, but her client was a bald-faced liar. She was itching to hold Ben's feet to the fire and make him explain his fake identities, hidden cash, and lies. Her fury lasted ten seconds before Quinn realized she couldn't ask Ben about his hidden cache without tipping her hand that she'd been in his house. He would complain to Meadows, which only fueled her fury.

"He killed that man, didn't he?" Alice asked.

"I'm not sure he did."

"But what if he did?" she persisted. "What if he saw me?"

"The law firm will put you someplace safe. Like a hotel, with a comfy bed and a big TV. How do pizza and in-room movies sound?"

Alice's eyes lit up. "I'll get my stuff out of the closet."

While Alice labored up the stairs to gather her things, Quinn called Meadows. "I found a homeless woman named Alice Whitlock in the college theater who claims she saw Ben here Sunday night after eleven o'clock."

"How believable is she?"

"I believe her, but there might be problems. She's elderly and looks like she's been on the streets for a while. She had a run-in with Deke Bystrom on Monday morning but swears she didn't tell him she saw Ben."

"If Bystrom knew that woman had seen Ben at the theater, you wouldn't have found her. He'd have her on ice somewhere because she'd be the key witness against Ben. I'll arrange a hotel for her and a woman to stay with her. Do you want me to send a car for her?"

"Yes, please." Quinn gave him the location of the theater parking lot.

"Martha will be there shortly with a client contract for Alice to sign."

Quinn knew why Meadows wanted Alice to sign a contract, just like she knew he would offer his services pro bono. If Alice was a client, all her conversations were privileged. "We'll be waiting. I'll send you the pictures I took of the crime scene."

Quinn went inside the janitor's closet to check if

Alice could have seen Ben clearly in the hallway. Even with the closet door open a small crack, Quinn had a good view of the hall. Alice had passed the first hurdle of being a reliable witness.

Alice finished stuffing a blanket in a plastic trash bag. She tried to carry the trash bag and a well-worn duffle bag and winced under the weight.

"Give me the heaviest one, and I'll carry it." Quinn took the duffle, which couldn't have weighed more than ten pounds, and swung it over her good shoulder.

Alice shuddered. "I don't want to walk past that room where he died."

They crossed the stage to the back door, and Quinn locked the theater door behind them. The wind had stilled, and the campus was covered in a blanket of new snow. "Do you remember anything about the room where you found the body?"

Alice looked at her, puzzled. "All I saw was a dead guy. There could have been a three-ring circus in there, and I wouldn't have known."

"You're right. Dumb question. Where did you go when you left the theater?"

"To the camp in the woods. It's not so bad. Just a lot of folks down on their luck. I got friends there."

Quinn took Alice to the lounge outside the drama department offices and asked her to wait while she returned the key.

When Quinn walked in, Sally wore her heavy coat and hoisted her purse over her shoulder. "Thank you for lending me the key."

Sally took the key and dropped it in her desk drawer. "I hope you found whatever you were looking for."

"I did. Do you know who has keys to the stage

door?"

"Questions, questions from you. Of course, I do. I'm in charge of checking the keys out. Everyone who works on a show gets a key."

"Do they return then after the show?"

Sally frowned and shook her head. "Not always, though I don't see that's your business. Why should I check them in only to turn around and check them out again? They're all going to work on the next show. It's a small group of kids." Sally sidestepped around Quinn. "Goodbye."

"Wait, one last question. Do you know the last time the theater was cleaned?"

"Every Friday afternoon like clockwork." Sally made a show of wrapping her scarf over her lower face before she marched out.

Quinn collected Alice, and they walked toward the parking lot. "How did you get inside the theater Sunday night?"

"The door was open."

"Was it always open?"

"Sometimes, but I had a key," Alice mumbled. "I know I shouldn't have taken it, but I never stole anything else, and I'm not the only one with a key. Those kids leave all kinds of stuff lying around. They'd leave their kidneys on a table if they weren't inside them."

"Did you lock the door behind you?"

Alice frowned. "No, I leave it like I find it."

They took shelter from the snow under the eaves of a building, and Quinn explained to Alice who Martha was and that Mr. Meadows was sending a contract he needed her to sign so he could help her.

"I don't have any money."

"He not charging you. We need your help, and you'll feel safer off the streets."

Quinn had allayed Alice's anxiety by the time Martha pulled into the parking lot and stopped beside them. Quinn opened the passenger side door. "Hi Martha, thanks for coming." Quinn helped Alice into the car and said, "Martha will take good care of you."

"Hello, Alice," Martha said. "I thought you might need a hot cup of coffee on a cold day like this." She handed Alice a to-go cup. "And there's a box of fresh donuts on the backseat."

Alice was all smiles.

"Do you know where the firm is putting her up?" Quinn asked Martha.

"It's the Microtel on Thornton Avenue. Sarah Bradford will be her minder. I'll send you her number."

"Thanks." Quinn told Alice, "I'll see you after you get settled. I know Sarah and you will get along great."

She watched them drive off before calling the director of Hope House. Quinn had worked with her on a complex child custody case a year ago. If Alice was a regular at the shelter, someone might remember if she tried to get a bed on Sunday night.

After exchanging pleasantries, Quinn said, "I'm working a case and ran into Alice Whitlock. Do you know her?"

"I do," the director said. "Alice is such a sweet old dear. She ended up on the streets after her son passed and his disability payments stopped."

"She looks like she had some tough times. Alice is a witness in a murder case I'm working on. Do you know if she tried to get a bed there on Sunday night?"

"Wait a minute. I have to pull the file up. We make

everyone sign in who comes through the door. Yes, Alice signed in right as we were closing. We were full, and we had to turn her away. Is she okay?"

"Yes, she's staying with a friend of mine. Will you hang onto the list in case we need it?"

"No problem. We keep them all in a computer file."

Now, it was time to talk with Ben.

Chapter 14

It was nearly six in the evening when Quinn called Ben. "Where are you? We need to talk."

"At the Bluebird Theater. I just signed the papers and got the keys. What's up?"

"I'm on my way."

"Don't come here. There's no heat in the building. I'll meet you at the Starlight. Park in the alley and come in the back door. I'll be waiting in my office."

She knew Ben would be his usual charming and charismatic self, but she wasn't falling for it tonight. Quinn had let her feelings about him cloud her perspective. There was no chance of that tonight, not after what she'd learned.

When she entered the bar's back door, she heard the band belting out tunes and the crowd singing along. Ben poked his head out of his office. "There you are. Thought I heard the back door close." He smiled, and she pushed aside the familiar warm tug she felt when she saw him.

When Ben stood to the side for her to enter his office, Quinn felt the heat from his hand on the small of her back and the strong, almost magnetic attraction to Ben. It was as though the universe was pulling her to him.

"Have a seat." Instead of sitting behind his desk, he sat next to her. She could see the concern on his face. "Would you like a drink?"

"No, thank you." Even to her, her voice sounded cold.

"Quinn, whatever you've come to say, just tell me. We can handle it."

"There's nothing for us to handle. You lied to me and your lawyer. A witness saw you coming out of the Green Room Sunday night. She picked your picture out of a lineup."

Ben lowered his head and pinched the bridge of his nose. "Okay, I was there. I'm sorry. I was worried when I couldn't find Paul, and he wasn't answering his phone. I wish I hadn't seen him lying like that on the sofa. I'd sat there so often with him, and then to see him dead like that."

Quinn saw Ben's grief, and she felt a surge of hope. The police had held back the fact that Paul's body was found on the sofa to winnow out the crazies who called in and copped to every crime. Ben couldn't have known unless he was there. "When were you there?"

"Around eleven." He raised his head, and his gray eyes were wet with tears. "I'm sorry I lied to you. I hadn't seen Meadows since I was on my way to prison, and I'd never met you. I was afraid of what you'd think of me." He pulled himself upright and said, "I didn't kill my brother."

The upbeat music and voices of noisy patrons were a stark contrast to the quiet tension between them. "Tell me everything about that night," Quinn asked.

Ben put his elbows on his knees and rested his head in his hands. "Paul called around three o'clock on Sunday and said he was breaking up Magarite after rehearsal. She'd agreed to meet him at the theater. Paul said he'd had all the drama he could stomach. I was glad he would be out from under her influence and asked him to come to my house for a drink after it was over. He said he would be there by ten at the latest. It got to be late, and I was worried and called him. It went to voice mail, so I drove over to his house. It was locked and dark, and at first, I assumed he and Margarite were off somewhere having make-up sex, but I couldn't shake the sense that something was wrong. I went to the theater to look for him and found him dead." Ben searched her face for acceptance. "Do you believe me?"

He looked vulnerable and wounded. Quinn wanted to shout, *Yes, I believe you; let me hold you and share your grief.* But she couldn't. He'd lied to her and had unexplained documents and cash hidden in his kitchen. She gave him a moment to compose himself, then asked, "Did you pass the front of the theater on your way to the stage door?"

"No," he looked at her quizzically. "I parked behind the Starlight and walked through the woods."

"Did you know about the surveillance camera on the front?"

"Yes, because Paul griped that was the only camera the college would provide. I wasn't trying to avoid being seen. It takes the same time for me to walk from the bar to the theater as it does to fight traffic on Colfax and find parking on the campus. I always went to see Paul the back way."

"Did anyone at the Starlight see you leave and come back?"

"No, the bar is closed on Sunday night."

"Meadows will request the street cameras from the city."

"Good. You'll see my car turning into the alley

behind the bar." The first shock was easing, and Ben seemed stronger now.

"Was the stage door locked?"

He shook his head. "No, I couldn't have gotten in if it was. I don't have a key. Now, I have a question for you. Who saw me?"

"A homeless woman who was sleeping in a closet."

"I want to talk to her."

"Meadows has her tucked away so Bystrom can't talk to her again."

Ben paled. "Did she tell Bystrom about me?"

"Not yet, but we haven't imprisoned her. She could walk away anytime."

"Maybe Paul found her sleeping in the theater, and when he tried to boot her out, she killed him."

Quinn shook her head. "Paul died before ten. Alice arrived around ten-thirty. I checked her story out. She signed into a local shelter but was turned away because there weren't enough beds."

His jaw went slack. "Then she's my alibi. She confirmed that I was there after Paul was killed. This is good news, isn't it?"

"It could be. Alice is elderly and homeless, and she has to hold up under cross-examination by the cops and the District Attorney."

"Did Alice see Margarite?" Ben asked.

Quinn shook her head. "Were you at the theater earlier Sunday evening?"

He stiffened. "No, I wasn't."

Ben dragged his hand through his hair. "I saw the bottle of booze by him, but I figure there was more than booze in Paul's system when he died."

"His tox screen was positive for cocaine."

Ben sighed and rubbed his eyelids. "I'm not surprised. I don't want his reputation trampled in the mud. I don't want people to remember him as an addict. He was so much more than that, and he can't defend himself."

Ben looked shattered. Quinn believed he was telling the truth, but she couldn't trust him if she caught him in another lie.

"Paul was under a lot of stress even before Margarite started badgering him to get married. He had to do everything: raise money, shoo the homeless out, and even try to get the bat colony in the theater exterminated. It costs a fortune to keep the program afloat, and no one else lifted a finger to find donors. He couldn't go back to Mrs. Alderberry because she'd had a stroke, and her kids had taken over her affairs. They're guarding the family fortune like the Hounds of Hades. He didn't know how he would keep the department afloat without donations.

"Paul was a genius. All he wanted to do was write and direct. I begged him to take a sabbatical and get into rehab, but he wouldn't. Maybe he could have gotten his head on straight if I could have convinced him to get away."

"You can't blame yourself."

His voice became so soft Quinn had to lean in to hear him. "You don't understand. Paul was always there for me. I let him down when he needed me." Ben looked exhausted. The lines around his eyes had dug deep.

"You're grieving and tired. Go home and get some sleep." She stood and offered her hand. "I'll walk out with you."

Ben grasped her hand and held on. "Do you believe I'm innocent?"

"Yes."

"That means a lot to me." He held the back door open for her. A stinging wind was howling through the alley and whistling between the buildings. Snow was falling, and Ben said, "Looks like we'll have a white Christmas."

Quinn laughed. "At this rate, we'll be snowed in before Christmas."

He held the car door for her. "That wouldn't be so bad, would it?" Ben said with a crooked smile.

Quinn slid in and looked up at him. "No, it wouldn't." She turned the key, and the car struggled to start, making an irritating eh-eh-eh sound before it died. She tried once more with no luck.

Ben opened the car door. "Maybe it just needs a jump. I'll get my battery cables."

He pulled his car beside hers and attached the cables. After two failed attempts to start her car, he said, "I'm no mechanic and doubt you can get a tow in this weather. I'll give you a lift home and arrange a tow to your garage tomorrow."

"Thanks. I don't think my car is budging in this storm."

Ben held his hand on her back as they walked to his car. Quinn felt a storm of emotions; her body was humming with attraction. She had flutters in her stomach and was nervous and excited at the same time.

Chapter 15

Ben walked Quinn to her door. She hadn't left the porch light on and fumbled, trying to work the lock. Charley was inside whining and scratching. Ben took her keys, and when he opened the door, Charley bounced to him, skidded to stop, and wagged her tail.

"She's a beautiful dog. What breed is she?" Ben asked.

"She's a giant schnauzer and standard poodle mix."

Ben bent down and scratched Charley's ears and told her what a good girl she was. Suddenly, the dog was on her feet, her head low and growling. Ben grabbed her collar and held on.

Quinn looked around and saw two squad cars glide to a stop in front of the house. Deke Bystrom and two cops got out and walked up the drive.

The two patrol officers stood off the porch, legs apart and arms folded over their chests. Bystrom climbed the steps and stood by Quinn and Ben.

Charley rumbled deep in her throat. Ben kept a tight hold on her. "Can I help you?" he asked Bystrom.

Bystrom smirked. "My business is with Ms. Kane. Step aside and get that damn dog outta here. I have a warrant to search your home," Bystrom said to Quinn. "We're looking for anything pertinent to the murder of Paul Loughty."

"You won't find anything," Quinn said.

Bystrom brushed past her, and the patrolmen followed Bystrom into the house. Quinn was hard on their heels.

"If you don't have a lawyer, I'll call mine," Ben said as he hauled a protesting Charley toward the back door.

"I've got mine on speed dial," Quinn said. She was disappointed when she got Ed Adams's voicemail. *Really, could the man ever just answer his phone?* She left an urgent message.

Bystrom directed the officers to search her bedroom. He stuck by her side as though he thought she might run. Seeing him in her home made her feel like her head would explode. When Ben returned to the house, she heard Charley howling in protest at being left out in the cold.

Bystrom crossed his arms over his chest and nodded toward Ben. "What's he doing here?" he asked Quinn. "Bet old man Meadows would love to know you're sleeping with the client. The state licensing board might get a call, too, probably an ethics violation, another mark against your license."

"Ms. Kane had car trouble, and I drove her home," Ben said through gritted teeth.

"Ah, hmm. Car trouble, and you call her Ms. Kane. Likely story," Bystrom said. He stepped close to Quinn, so close she could see his nose hairs needed trimming. "Where's your weapon?"

"I have a permit to carry. You know already know that."

Bystrom made the gimme gesture with his hand.

"I'm going to reach behind me and pull it out slowly."

"Hand it over," Bystrom said.

"I'm going to unload it first." Quinn popped the cylinder, removed the bullets, and handed it to Bystrom butt first. "You know that isn't the gun that killed Paul Loughty. The murder weapon was a twenty-two, and that's a thirty-eight-caliber pistol."

Bystrom made a show of putting her gun in an evidence bag and labeling it.

Quinn was still doing a slow burn when an officer came out of her office holding a brown paper bag out to Bystrom. "Sir, we found this taped to the wall behind the desk."

Bystrom snatched the bag and opened it. "Look what we have here. The same caliber gun as the one that killed Loughty. The perfect weapon for a woman your size, lightweight and small enough to conceal on your body. I bet we'll find your prints on it."

"She had no reason to kill my brother," Ben snapped angrily.

A uniform stepped between Ben and Bystrom.

Bystrom looked at Quinn. "I'll charge your boyfriend with obstruction if he doesn't get control of himself."

"A bit odd, isn't it?" Quinn was red-faced and full-on mad. "A murder weapon you haven't been able to find turns up in my house right after a couple of goons came by to warn me off the case. It was planted, and you know it. You have a history of evidence tampering."

Ben stepped to her side and touched her arm. "Don't say anything else until you have a lawyer."

Bystrom seemed very pleased with himself. "I think we should continue this conversation at the station." He took Quinn's elbow and led her out the door. Ben followed behind them.

They nearly bumped into Trixie on the porch. "What's going on?"

"Will you take care of Charley?" Quinn asked.

"Sure. Do you need me to call anyone?"

"Call Ed Adams. Ben's going with me to the station."

At the mention of the station, Trixie's eyes were as big as saucers. Ben rattled off his phone number to Trixie. "Call me if you can't get in touch with Adams."

Bystrom marched Quinn across the yard. He opened the back of the squad car and lightly touched the top of her head as she got in.

"Where are you taking her?" Ben asked Bystrom.

"Midtown station."

Ben called to Quinn. "I'm right behind you. I'll have a lawyer there as soon as possible."

Bystrom slammed the car door, and the driver was moving away from the curb before she could thank Ben.

****

Quinn sat alone in the interview room. Adams hadn't arrived, but she knew Ben and Trixie wouldn't disappoint her. They would get a lawyer.

She had plenty of time to think. Though Bystrom kept his job after the Internal Affairs investigation of the Nelson case, the stigma stuck with him. He'd never been promoted; even his godfather couldn't fix that. But now, Bystron thought he'd found a way to pay her back for what he'd called her meddling in the Nelson case. Her prints weren't on the gun, but its presence in her house would be a problem.

The interview door banged open, and Ed Adams walked in escorted by a uniformed officer. Ed waited until they were alone to say, "There's a guy out front,

Ben Loughty, who told me to tell you he's waiting for you."

She was right about Ben. He was someone she could count on.

Ed sat across the table from her. "What's this about a murder investigation and a weapon found in your house?"

"I've been framed."

She started to explain the warning and how she found the open window but didn't have time to finish before Bystrom and a uniformed cop strode inside and made a show of noisily pulling out their chairs. They sat opposite Quinn and Ed.

"You want to tell us about the gun, Ms. Kane?" Bystrom began.

"I've never seen the gun before."

"We found it hidden in your house."

Quinn stole a look at Ed. He had his poker face on.

"Who are you protecting?" Bystrom asked.

"No one."

"Your boyfriend had a reason to kill Paul Loughty."

"He's a client, not a boyfriend, and there's no evidence he killed his brother."

"Says you," Bystrom said.

Adams sat back and steepled his fingers. "My client denies the gun is hers and denies any knowledge of the murder of Paul Loughty. Stop this charade and charge her or let her go."

"I think she knows a lot more than she's telling us," Bystrom said. He crossed his arms over his chest and told Quinn, "You could go down for murder."

"Without evidence, you're wasting my client's time," Adams said.

Additional posturing and chest-beating occurred before Detective Bystrom stood and told Quinn, "You're free to go." But he called after Quinn as she and Adams left, "We'll be talking to you again."

Ben was waiting for her in the crowded area near the desk sergeant. He leaped to his feet when he saw her, and when Adams offered to drive her home, Ben rushed to say he would drive her.

"Let's step outside," Adams said. Ben and Quinn followed him until they were well away from the building. "I'd like a moment alone with my client," he told Ben.

"He can stay," Quinn said.

"All right," Adams said. "You're not telling me everything. I can't do my best unless I know. I'm a good lawyer and can handle whatever you're holding back. Call my office when you're ready to talk."

Quinn watched Adams walk away, uncertain that Adams could handle a powerful man like Logan Latham and a dirty cop like Deke Bystrom.

Ben put his arm around her shoulders and walked Quinn to his car. He opened the door for her. She scooted onto the plush leather seat, leaned her head back on the headrest, and closed her eyes.

Ben got in and turned the heater on high. "I think you need a more experienced lawyer than Ed Adams. I'd be happy to suggest someone."

Quinn held up a hand to protest.

"We can talk about it tomorrow," he said. "Tonight has been rough on you."

Quinn also thought she needed better legal advice but would have to rob a bank to pay one. She didn't even have equity in her home anymore.

When Ben parked in her driveway, Trixie must have been watching because she burst out of her front door, ran over, and grabbed Quinn in a bear hug. "I've been so worried." She looked at Ben and stuck out her hand. "I'm Trixie Knight, from next door. We didn't have time to get acquainted earlier."

"Ben Loughty," he said, shaking her hand. "I'm glad Quinn has a friend nearby."

Ben unlocked the front door and stood aside for the women to enter. Quinn went in first and called Charley's name.

"I took her to my house," Trixie said. "She was crazy upset when you and the cops left. I'll get her."

Trixie raced to her house and returned with Charley bounding at her heels. Quinn bent down and hugged her pup. Once everyone was inside, Ben locked the front door and joined the women in the living room. He sat by Quinn while she told Trixie about Bystrom finding the murder weapon in her house. Now that the shock had worn off, Quinn felt energized by the rage roiling through her. She had to bring Bystrom down, keep her freedom, and find Paul's killer. A tall order for a woman with a murder weapon found in her house.

"It's time we nail this guy's ass to the wall," Quinn said. She had been digging into the Bystroms' finances and explained what she'd discovered about their lifestyle. "Bystrom didn't buy his mansion in a ritzy neighborhood north of the river and two luxury cars on his cop salary. His wife has a clothes boutique in an upscale strip mall, but unless she's making money hand over fist selling dresses, Bystrom's dirty. I need proof he's on the take. It will be even sweeter if we tie him to Logan Latham."

Trixie beamed. "What fun. It was getting boring at work."

"What's the risk if you get caught?" Ben asked Trixie.

Trixie answered, "I won't get caught because I've been trained by the best snoops in the business. I work with people in the FBI, Homeland Security, and the IRS. I can turn his life inside out." Trixie got up and hugged Quinn. "I can't wait to get started. You need to get some rest. Call me tomorrow."

Quinn sank back into the sofa cushions. She'd set a firestorm under Bystrom, which was a good day's work, and Trixie was right. She was tired.

Charley whined and nudged Ben's hand. He cupped the dog's face in his hands. "Such a good girl. Is she hungry?"

"Yes, the dog food is under the sink. Will you feed her?"

"Of course. Come on, girl."

Quinn could hear Ben pouring kibble into Charley's bowl.

"Have you eaten?" he asked from the kitchen.

"I'm not hungry."

She heard him rummage in the cabinets and water running. In a few minutes, Ben brought her a cup of coffee. "Drink this and warm up." Charley padded quietly behind him and laid by Quinn's feet.

Quinn wrapped both hands around the mug and let the heat soak into her palms.

Ben sat across from her, sipping his coffee from her favorite mug, which seemed fitting.

The adrenaline rush had faded, and Quinn was about to nod off when Charley whimpered in her sleep, and her front legs pawed the floor. Quinn rubbed her soft fur, and the dog quieted. She looked up at Ben. "Thank you for going to the station. I owe you an explanation."

"You don't owe anything."

Quinn pulled her feet up under and looked at Ben over the rim of her mug. "Bystrom and I have a long history. None of it is good." She told him about the Nelson case and the internal affairs investigation. "Bystrom lodged a complaint with my licensing board." She explained the unrecorded interview with Margarite. "I didn't misrepresent myself."

"I don't believe you did. What does Logan Latham have to do with Bystrom?"

"He's Bystrom's godfather. He pulls the strings to keep him on the force, and Bystrom does favors for him. I shouldn't have told you all this. It's unprofessional."

"You and I have a mutual adversary, Deke Bystrom."

Their phones pinged at the same time. "There's a weather alert." Ben read from his phone. "Heavy snow and a travel advisory for the city."

A gust of wind rattled the house. Quinn went to the window and looked out. "It's snowing so hard I can't see past two feet from the house."

"I'd better get going, "Ben said.

She turned around and looked at him like he was crazy. "You can't drive in this. Get over here and look out the window."

He joined her and saw the whiteout.

"No way you'd make it out of the neighborhood. The plows won't get to the side streets for hours. You can stay here."

"Are you sure?"

"Yes."

"All right then. I'll build a fire in case we lose power."

"There's dry wood on the back porch."

Soon, Ben had a fire blazing. The wind gusted down the chimney and blew embers on the tile hearth, but the house was warm and cozy. Ben had opened a bottle of wine. The alcohol loosened Quinn's tongue. She told Ben about the foreclosure and that she and Charley were moving into an apartment.

"I'll lend you the money to pay off the loan."

"You know I can't take it. You're a client."

"I'm more than a client."

The power blinked off, and the only light came from the fire. Ben looked out the window. "Power's off in the neighborhood."

Suddenly, Quinn felt embarrassed she had confided in him. He'd been a good listener, but she'd stepped out of line talking to him. And she was making a habit of crossing the line with him. She took her wine glass to the kitchen. "I'll get you a blanket and pillow and leave fresh towels in the bathroom. I'm going to shower and go to bed."

When she returned with the blanket, Ben had already slipped off his shoes and unbuttoned his shirt. She stared at his sculpted body and mussed hair, thinking, *what if?*

Ben took the blanket from her. His hand grazed her arm, and she felt a frisson of desire. "Good night," she managed to say.

Quinn stood in the hot shower, luxuriating in the water, beating down her shoulders and neck. The warm water brought her tight shoulders down from under her ears, and she relaxed. She wondered if Ben slept in the raw and what it would feel like to lay in his arms.

Chapter 16

Quinn woke to the smell of coffee and sat upright in bed, startled until she remembered Ben had spent the night. She pulled on her robe and took the time to brush her hair.

Ben was in the kitchen making toast with Charley sitting at his feet and gazing lovingly up at him. His dark hair was still wet from the shower, and she smelled the scent of her soap on his skin. An image of him naked flashed through her mind. *Really,* she scolded herself. *This has to stop.*

"Good morning."

He turned around and smiled. "Charley nudged me awake when the power came on. I fed her. I hope we didn't wake you." Ben poured her a mug of coffee and set a plate of toast in front of her."

"Charley usually has me out of bed by this time."

Ben joined her at the small table. He shoved a lock of hair off his forehead. "I have to leave soon to meet with my builder. I don't think you're safe here. I have room at my place."

He had one bed in his apartment. Neither of them would be safe.

Ben held up one hand to ward off her weighing in. "You can have the bedroom, and I'll take the sofa."

"I won't let anyone run me out of my home," Quinn blurted, then laughed, realizing that was precisely what was happening. "Well, not until Logan Latham forecloses on my house, and we have to leave. I'll bunk in with Trixie if I need to. Thanks, we'll be fine."

Quinn was suddenly self-conscious. What if Meadows found out Ben had spent the night? It was bad enough that she had to tell her boss about the search warrant and being hauled in for questioning.

As though he was a mind reader, Ben said, "Meadows will never know about last night unless you choose to tell him."

Quinn thought, *what is it about this man that he always says the perfect thing?*

Ben checked the time and rose. "I'm going to be late if I don't get a move on." He rinsed his coffee cup in the sink. "I've arranged a rental car to be delivered here in the next half hour and for your car to be towed to the shop."

She followed him to the door. "Thank you for staying last night."

Ben leaned over and kissed her forehead. "It was an honor to be by your side."

Quinn gazed after him, still feeling his warm kiss. If they had met under other circumstances, if he hadn't lied to her, if he wasn't a murder suspect, if she hadn't found the cash and fake passports in his house, if he wasn't posh and she ordinary, then maybe *nothing.* Only a fool would think it wouldn't ever work.

Quinn dumped her coffee in the sink and headed to get dressed. A week ago, she had thought of herself as a rising young professional with a bright future. Now, her reputation was in tatters; she was losing her home, and there was a threat to her license. Worse was the foreboding sense that it wasn't over. She was scrambling as fast as she could to duck, weave, and respond to the threats, but she didn't know how much more she could take.

Then, she remembered what her grandmother said when times were hard. *There's nothing here that I can't do.* It seemed like an appropriate mantra for the morning, and Quinn mumbled it twice before she brushed her teeth.

Quinn remembered to get her spare gun from the top of her closet before she left. As much as she wanted to get the meeting with Meadows over, it was too early for him to be in the office. She had to do something constructive while she waited for her boss to bawl her out.

Lenny Mishler was the only person she was sure was awake. He was still in the hospital, probably eating breakfast and reading the newspaper. As shop foreman, he had a ringside seat to the goings-on in the Green Room, and she hoped he would be in the mood to talk about it.

Quinn found Lenny on the cardiac floor, in a room far enough from the nurse's station to slip inside unseen. Flowers covered every surface, and the overly sweet smell masked the scent of the hospital. Lenny was a slim, wiry man with thinning gray hair, a small turned-up nose, and a weak chin. He was propped up in bed with his half-eaten breakfast tray. An array of lines, leads, and tubes snaked out of his body.

"Who are you?" he asked, looking up from his food.

She smiled. "I'm Quinn Kane, an investigator with the Meadows law firm. We represent Dr. Loughty's estate." She extended her hand. "Do you feel up to talking?"

His palm was rough with calluses. "I feel happy to be on this side of the dirt. The good Lord wasn't ready to bring me home Monday morning. Pull up a chair."

Quinn scooted the visitor's chair closer to the bed. "I'm glad you're feeling better."

"Me, too. I already talked to the cops and set them straight about finding the stage door open Monday morning. I locked it on Friday afternoon. It should have been locked, and you know who the problem is? It's Sally. She likes to be liked. She kowtows to the kids so they'll hang around and talk to her. She's the one who checks out the keys and doesn't get them returned. Everyone and his dog have a key to the theater. It's a disgrace. I've told her for years that she needs to get those keys back. Maybe now that Dr. Loughty was murdered, she'll listen to reason."

The number of unaccounted keys was a nightmare for Quinn, along with having no surveillance on the back of the theater. But it was helpful to Meadows. He could argue that any one of the unknown people with keys could have come through the woods to the theater and murdered Paul. "I can see how not knowing who has keys would be a security problem. When was the last time you saw the Green Room before you found Paul's body?"

"Right after five o'clock on Friday. I wait until the cleaners leave, and then I check every space to make sure they did their job before I secure the building."

"So the Green Room was clean?"

He sniffed. "They'd mopped the floor, but that's about all. There was still trash on the tables, and it smelled like an ash can. The drama kids use it as their private hangout. It's like their little clubhouse, and it's always a mess. Dr. Loughty didn't make them clean up after themselves, and I know for a fact he gave the cleaners hell if they interrupted him when he was using the room."

Mishler pulled himself into a sitting position without making any alarms or buzzers ring. "Let me say this right off. I told Dr. Beckett what Paul and his students were doing in the theater more than once, and Beckett blew me off like I was some Bible-toting fool. I knew why he protected Paul. Paul made him look good. He brought in the money that kept the department going. In my book, that makes Beckett as guilty as Paul."

Quinn heard the clatter of the breakfast trays loaded on the service carts and hoped they wouldn't come in until she finished talking with Lenny. "Guilty of what?"

"Paul and the kids were using drugs and partying half-naked. I'm a God-fearing man. I couldn't believe Beckett wouldn't put a stop to it."

Quinn glanced at the cardiac monitor. It was making the same squiggly lines it had when she arrived. No warnings beeped, and Mishler showed no signs he was anywhere near through talking. He seemed as keen to speak as Sally and Knupp had been. Except Lenny's story was very different from theirs. It was like they were describing two different men. "Do you have evidence to back up what you thought was happening in the theater?"

"Of course, I have evidence. Nobody knew what I was doing until the technology people found my little camera feed running on the college's server about a week ago. I was feeding the video from the camera in the Green Room to the computer in my office. That's how they tracked it to me. They barged into my office and took my camera and my laptop. Said it all belonged to the college, and they could take it."

That explained the patch on the wall and the fresh paint.

"Do you have any of the video?"

Lenny smiled. "Sure do. I have a clip saved on my phone. That's what I showed Dr. Beckett last Friday."

"How did he react?"

"He fired me on the spot. I was supposed to be out of my office and turn in my keys by noon on Monday. I hope they let me get back in there and get what's mine. If they don't, the look on Beckett's face when I showed him that video was worth losing some of my personal tools. He can't deny that he knows what happened because I sent the Dean a copy of the video while I was at it. Too bad I won't be there when Beckett gets the ax, but I'm glad to be out of that Sodom and Gomorrah."

Quinn wondered if Beckett had been angry enough to kill Paul after discovering his Golden Boy had become a liability. "Who do you think killed Paul?"

"I don't know. Wasn't one of the other professors. They didn't like him, but killing Paul would have been like killing the goose that laid the golden eggs. We'd all have been looking for jobs."

"Did you know that Paul was in a relationship with Margarite Mancini?"

Lenny snort-laughed and wiped his nose on his scrub top. "Of course I did. He was always in bed with one student or another. He promised to jumpstart their acting careers if they had sex with him. I heard him tell a girl he could get her on stage with a professional troupe in New York. Paul said he had a friend there and swore he could get her a spot in a play. He'd promise those girls the moon to get in their panties."

"Did he ever place a student with a professional theater group?"

"Not that I ever heard about."

"Do you think a student might have killed him?"

He shrugged. "Dunno know. It could have been anybody with all those keys floating around. I think Paul had people who needed him, but I don't think he had any friends. I didn't like him, but I sure as hell didn't kill him. My missus and I celebrated our anniversary at Chinese Charlie's on Sunday night. Forty-eight years we've been together. You can check it out. I got us a reservation at the restaurant."

Having a reservation didn't mean he was there Sunday night. Still, a phone call to the manager or a credit card receipt would do nicely as an alibi. "Did you ever meet Dr. Loughty's brother Ben?"

"Sure, I did. Ben used to come around to see Paul. The Loughtys.ggg,. were a well-known family. I grew up here and knew Ben had been in prison. All that stuff was in the papers. But it looks to me like Ben turned out okay. Always nice and respectful when we talked. He didn't like what was going on. I heard him talking to Paul about it. I'm right next door, and those walls aren't soundproofed."

"Do you remember what Ben said?"

"He told Paul he needed to stop doing this crap and get into rehab."

"How did Paul take it?"

"He laughed and told Ben not to worry about him. Told Ben he should lighten up. After that, Ben quit coming around the theater, and I admire him for it. Shows he's got some gumption."

Before Quinn could ask another question, a nurse

came in and looked daggers at Quinn. "It's not visiting hours. You'll have to leave."

"Yes, of course," Quinn said. "I was on my way out. Mr. Mishler, would you email me a copy of that video?" She handed him her card.

"Sure thing."

****

Quinn was idling in traffic on her way to the office, wondering if Mishler was a voyeur. Maybe he had been titillated by rumors of sex and drugs in the Green Room and installed the camera so he could watch. She'd never know what motivated Mishler to set the camera, but he had undoubtedly stirred the pot.

Traffic was moving at the speed of a racewalker, and she had plenty of time to think about the case. After Dr. Beckett saw Mishler's video on Friday afternoon, Beckett knew his job was in jeopardy. When Paul's body was found in the Green Room, Beckett must have been chewing his nails. He knew the Green Room was where the action was and that the sex scandal would break wide open.

Mishler's video would work its way up the chain of command at the college from the dean to the Board of Regents, everyone hoping it never leaked to the press until they'd had time to spin the story of their innocence. But it wouldn't happen like they wanted. Too many people were involved for the scandal to stay a secret. Someone with an ax to grind would leak the footage to the media, sit back, and watch the mayhem unfold.

After talking to Mishler, Quinn was positive the blood trail was made after rehearsal and before Mishler found the body. The police would be certain, too. They'd come for a blood sample from Ben. Good thing that

Meadows had the foresight to send samples of his blood and blood from the crime scene to the Bharat Lab. Alice's testimony that Ben was at the theater after the murder wasn't enough. The lab results would either indict Ben or vindicate him.

Quinn wondered if Bystrom would require a blood sample from the rest of the suspects who didn't have air-tight alibis. Margarite claimed to be alone Sunday night. Tiberius and Wilkerson alibied each other. Beckett's wife alibied him. Knupp said he was alone in his office until Roxie came by. Mishler said he was at the restaurant. While Quinn hadn't received a call back from Emily Halmstad, she had a settlement offer. All Emily had to do was sign the papers and walk away with the check. Most likely, she hadn't felt the need to shoot Paul.

What Quinn needed was the surveillance video from Sunday night. She had only Roxie's word about what happened after rehearsal. At the next intersection, Quinn pulled over and called the chief of the college's security department. She offered to swing by and pick up a copy of the footage. To her surprise, he was apologetic. "We're stretched thin here with the murder inquiry. I'm sorry. I should have already done it. Give me your email, and I'll send it to you as soon as we get off the phone."

When Quinn arrived at the law firm, everyone was busy. Paralegals dashed from office to office, delivering stacks of files. Two associates were meeting with a client in the small conference room. If Meadows were here, he'd hear the sweet ka-ching of money being made. Martha was on the phone, and Quinn waited to talk to her. When she hung up, Quinn asked her when Meadows would be in.

"He's meeting with a judge at the courthouse. He

won't be much longer."

"Would you let me know when he arrives?"

"Sure thing."

Quinn went to her office and checked her phone messages. The PI in California had been in touch and left a message. On the night Paul was killed, his son, Jason, had worked at an art show in the Whittier College Gallery. Paul's ex-wife, her plastic surgeon husband, and their nine-year-old son had been vacationing at the Royal Hawaiian Hotel in Honolulu. The only family member in town was her client.

Next, Quinn called the restaurant where Lenny Mishler said he celebrated his anniversary. She reached an assistant manager who worked Sunday night and remembered Mishler's special request to have flowers on the table before he and his wife arrived. He remembered because the flowers were delivered late, and he didn't get them to the table until after the Mishlers were seated. Lenny hadn't been happy about it.

While Quinn had been on the phone with the restaurant, Mishler's email arrived with the video attached. She downloaded it and watched Paul partying with his students in the Green Room. One couple was drunk dancing and tumbled to the floor, and to the delight of the others, they peeled off their clothes. As the party wound down, Paul and Margarite were alone on the sofa, undressing each other as fast as possible. Paul sat behind her, fondling her breasts as she snorted the first line of coke from the coffee table. Paul took his turn, and then Margarite pulled him down on top of her.

No wonder Beckett had looked worried the first time she'd talked to him. Even though the video couldn't be entered as evidence at a trial because Mishler had no right to make the recording, it was damning evidence of Beckett's leadership.

Martha buzzed her that Meadows was in his office.

When Quinn walked into his office, she noticed how tired and angry Meadows looked. Did he already know what happened last night? She decided to take control of the situation before he could question her. "Last night, the police served a warrant and searched my house. They found a twenty-two caliber pistol hidden in my office."

"Is it yours?"

No, I've never seen it before."

"Is it the gun that killed Paul?"

"It could be."

"Do you have an attorney?" The questions came rapid-fire—like she was on the witness stand at a trial.

"Yes, Ed Adams."

"You need a criminal defense attorney. Meadows kneaded his eyelids with his fingertips in a familiar sign he was losing patience. "Hire one."

"Yes, sir." She left his office, knowing she was skating on thin ice. If the powerful James Meadows fired her, she'd never work as an investigator again.

Chapter 17

Quinn sat in her office, hoping what just happened would be the nadir of her career. She couldn't image much worse befalling her than being suspected of murder.

She wasn't ready to dump Ed Adams yet. Maybe he could pull a rabbit out of his hat, and perhaps she could find Paul's killer. Then, she wouldn't need a criminal attorney. Stranger things had happened, right?

Quinn called Doc Iverson, desperate for his opinion on the blood at the crime scene. When he answered his phone, she braced for a tongue-lashing because he was well known for not liking his work interrupted. He didn't disappoint her.

"I don't have that blood analysis you wanted. All you people expect miracles. Science takes time." He hung up on her, which kept her from snapping at him.

While Doc was haranguing her, she received a text. The police chief at the college had sent the surveillance video. Quinn texted Ben that she had the video and asked him to meet her at her office. She received an auto-respond text that he was in a meeting. Since she felt awkward after the kiss this morning, she needed some breathing space to sort out her feelings.

She downloaded the surveillance video file and watched the minutes and frames tick off at the top of each picture. She didn't notice any irregularities, but she'd ask

Meadows to send it to his forensic video expert. An expert would be able to determine if the footage was tampered with. If an amateur had tinkered with the video, she would see skips in the timecode, but an expert could cover his tracks too well for her to know.

She sped through the video from early Sunday morning to midafternoon. Light snow had fallen all morning. It had been a good day to stay inside and warm, and only a handful of people had passed the theater by three in the afternoon.

Shortly before four o'clock, Paul appeared, wrapped in a long coat and scarf. He turned on the sidewalk and walked toward the stage door, eventually putting him out of range of the front camera. Fifteen minutes after he arrived, Roxie came into view. Finally, at four-thirty, a young male and female walked together, chatting amicably, and disappeared behind the theater. Quinn assumed they were Todd and Melinda, the tech crew Roxie had mentioned.

There was no other activity until six-thirty. Todd and Melinda left the theater first. A few minutes later, Paul and Roxie appeared. They stopped to talk in front of the theater before Roxie peeled off toward Knupp's office, and Paul went in the opposite direction. Fifteen minutes later, Roxie reappeared, walking past the theater toward the Colfax train station. Roxie had given a good account of what happened on Sunday evening.

Quinn heard a knock on her door, looked up, and saw Ben. He dragged a chair over and sat beside her. "How did it go when you talked to Meadows?"

"He's not happy, but at least I told him before he found out from someone else." She bit her lip. She didn't want to tell Ben that Meadows told her to get a criminal defense attorney. Ben would offer to help pay. She had to do this her way.

She pointed at the screen and caught him up with what had happened. "Roxie, Paul, and two students arrived around four-thirty for rehearsal and left around six-thirty." She rewound the video to the frames that showed Todd and Melinda leaving. "These are the students. Do you know them?"

"I've never seen either of them before, but I quit going to the cast parties long ago."

Quinn played the clip of Roxie and Paul talking in front of the theater. "From here, Roxie went to Knupp's office. When I talked to Knupp earlier, he confirmed she brought material for her thesis to him Sunday night. Roxie took the train home from the Colfax station. I checked, and she did. Roxie said that Paul told her he was getting a sandwich and returning to the theater to work. We should see him return soon."

Quinn started the video. The frames rolled past with no sign of Paul. Then, at seven-fifteen, a heavy-set figure wearing a hoodie that hid the face walked in front of the camera and turned onto the sidewalk leading to the stage door.

"I can't tell if it's a man or a woman," Ben said. "Back it up."

Quinn reversed a few frames and played it frame by frame. The figure walked casually, arms swinging at their side. Suddenly, the figure turned around as though a noise had startled them, and the front camera caught the face. "It's a woman," Ben exclaimed.

Quinn studied the broad face with high cheekbones, wide-set eyes, and a rosebud mouth. "Do you know her?"

"Never saw her before. She's dressed like a homeless person. Maybe she's heading to the camp."

The woman turned her back on the camera and disappeared into the shadows at the rear of the building. "If she has a key, she could be inside." Ben fidgeted. "The waiting is terrible. We know Paul's on his way back." He was about to say something else when he pointed to the screen. Paul was striding to the stage door, carrying a bag from a popular sandwich shop.

Quinn watched anger and grief flash across Ben's face. She felt like she was watching a suspenseful movie and wanted to tell Paul, *don't go inside*.

Paul disappeared behind the theater at seven thirty-one. They waited in tense silence for something to happen. Ben couldn't sit still, and Quinn was chewing the inside of her cheek, a nervous habit left over from childhood. When she thought she'd scream, a figure limped out of the shadows, heading to the front of the building.

"Who's that?" Ben leaned in close to the screen.

"I can't tell," Quinn said. A watch cap was pulled low on the forehead, nearly to the eyebrows, and an oversized calf-length coat came almost to the ankles. Quinn glanced away long enough to scribble seven forty-two in her notes. When the figure walked into the range of the front camera, Quinn exclaimed, "It's the same woman."

Ben pointed to the screen. "That's an expensive sheepskin coat she's wearing, and look," he said, pointing at her legs. "She's limping."

Quinn wondered if the woman had killed Paul, found him dead, or never went inside the theater. It was all speculation since no camera was on the back of the building. All she was sure of was that the woman had gone to the back of the building and returned dressed differently and limping. Nobody left an expensive coat and hat lying around in the dead of winter. Someone else was back there, but who would give up their coat in a winter storm?

Ben pointed at the screen. "She was inside with Paul long enough to kill him."

Quinn was as frustrated as Ben. "We don't know that she went inside the theater, only that she was near the stage door. She was out of the range of the camera for twenty-seven minutes. She could have walked to Colfax or the homeless camp and come back."

"She's suspicious as hell. She's the only person besides Paul we've seen since rehearsal ended. When she reappears, she's wearing different clothes and limps. Looks to me like she did something that made her want to change her appearance."

"We'll find her or whoever she got the coat from. Someone at the school or in the camp might recognize her." Quin sent a still frame of the woman to her phone. She restarted the video, and they watched the woman walk out of the camera's range toward the parking lot. Ten minutes passed.

Then, Margarite appeared.

Quinn sucked in her breath. "She lied to me."

Ben looked at her, a grim smile on his face. "I told you she was a good actress."

They watched Margarite battle the fierce wind as she made her way to the rear of the theater. Quinn was chewing the inside of her cheek again. Would Margarite find Paul dead or alive?

Nearly four minutes passed before they saw

Margarite tear out of the shadows, running pell-mell to the front of the theater.

"She killed him," Ben said.

Quinn wasn't so sure. Margarite could be running away because she found Paul dead. "She was out of view for less than four minutes. If she murdered him, she had to get inside, walk into the Green Room, shoot Paul twice at close range, and reappear halfway up the sidewalk. That's not much time to accomplish all that, and I don't see blood on her clothes."

"It's possible, and you know it. This is lousy black-and-white footage. She could be hosed in blood, and we couldn't tell. She's running like a banshee because she murdered him."

Ben was vulnerable, and his emotions were riding high. He was watching the last few moments of his brother's life. "You're not objective about Margarite," she said gently. "The other woman was out of sight for twenty-seven minutes. If she went inside, she had time to lie in wait for Paul."

"What would the unknown woman gain? I can't imagine she even knew Paul, and how did she know Paul would be there on Sunday night? He told me he was meeting Margarite, and she lied to you about it. Bystrom has the video, doesn't he?"

Quinn nodded. "I'm sure he's seen it."

"Why isn't she in jail?"

"Because, at this point, the police can't place Margarite inside the theater. I'm going to talk to her, and I'm going alone. She's a hostile witness. Mr. Meadows would tell you the same thing." Though Quinn was sure that Ed Adams would tell her not to talk to Margarite again.

Quinn figured Bystrom had already questioned Margarite a second time. The girl must have concocted a story believable enough for Bystrom, but he was bent and dangerous to Ben's freedom.

"I'm not going to sit around and do nothing," Ben said. "Send me a copy of the unknown woman's photo. I'll take it to the college and see if anyone recognizes her."

"Good," Quinn said. "Because we need to find her before some eager cop on Bystrom's team finds her and stashes her away like Meadows has hidden Alice."

"I'm going with you to talk to Alice," Ben said. "I know you'll ask her if she knows the woman on the video."

Quinn shook her head. She knew Alice would never talk if she brought Ben around. "We'll catch up later today."

After Ben left, she fast-forwarded the video until the time code reached midnight. No one else had come past the front of the theater. She emailed Meadows the video file and asked him to send it to the forensic expert. While the surveillance video didn't prove either woman killed Paul, a skilled lawyer like him could lead the jury like a donkey to a carrot to conclude that two women were there Sunday night and either could have killed Paul.

Quinn dropped by Martha's desk to tell her she would be out of the office most of the day. "You can reach me on my cell."

"Will do," Martha said. "I'm waiting for the company to send us the download link for the facial recognition software you wanted. I'll text you the minute it comes in."

Quinn might be able to put a name on the unknown

woman after she confronted Margarite Mancini.

****

Quinn knocked on Margarite's door. When she answered, Quinn was surprised to see the girl had lost weight from an already slender frame. The stress zit the girl was picking on her chin was the size of a dime.

"May I come in? I have some pictures to show you," Quinn said.

"Sure, come in." Margarite waved her in with a languid shrug of one shoulder.

Quinn picked her way through the clothes tossed on the floor and sat in the same chair she had on her earlier visit. She laid her phone on a small table. "You don't mind if I record the meeting, do you? Just so there won't be any confusion, I'm Quinn Kane with the Meadows Law Firm, investigating the death of Paul Loughty."

Margarite looked confused. "Whatever."

Quinn smiled to herself. She was right; Margarite knew nothing about the complaint to the licensing board. It was Bystrom's work.

Quinn took her time, setting out the time-stamped pictures of Margarite arriving and leaving the theater. "You were there on Sunday night."

The girl's face went chalk white. "Paul was dead when I found him. Oh my God, I swear it's true. He asked me to meet him after rehearsal, and I found him like that."

"Why did you lie?"

"I was terrified."

"Why didn't you call the police?"

"I didn't know what to do. I was afraid they'd think I killed him. I came home and started drinking, and I must have passed out. When I woke up the next morning,

I couldn't go to the police. It was too late. How could I explain that I'd left Paul alone in the theater all night?"

"Have you come clean and told the police you were there?"

"Oh yes, Detective Bystrom came by to talk to me again. He was so sweet about it when I explained the pictures. He said he knew I was in shock when he questioned me right after Paul died." Margarite's eyes were guileless. "He knew I was grieving and that I would remember things later. Now, it's all come back to me. I saw Ben that night. He made good on his threats. It's just all so, so tragic. Paul tried to straighten Ben out when they were kids, but he couldn't, and now my Paul is dead."

"Tell me about seeing Ben on Sunday night." Quinn kept her voice neutral.

Margarite slipped into the role of an important witness. "When I walked around the corner to the stage door, I saw him come out of the theater wiping blood off his hands on his pants. He looked like a crazy man. I must have screamed because he took off running into the woods. I nearly peed my pants when he turned around and looked over his shoulder at me before he disappeared."

"So, you saw a crazy guy with blood on his hands and still went inside the theater?"

Margarite grabbed some tissues and blew her nose. She took her time, milking the suspense for all she could. "I had to be brave. I knew I had to go in and check on Paul. He could have been hurt and needed my help, but my sweet Paul was gone." She cupped her flat belly and cried a gut-wrenching sound of anguish worthy of a theatrical performance. "What's going to happen to our baby?"

Quinn ignored her question. "Why was Ben threatening Paul?"

"He wanted money to bail out that stupid club of his, and Paul wouldn't give it to him. You don't know Ben like I do. He's a druggie, and he got my man hooked on drugs. I'll swear to it in court. I heard him threaten to kill Paul more than once. Now, my baby's fatherless."

Quinn put the picture of the mystery woman on the table. "Do you know this person?" She then tapped her finger on the time and date stamp. "She was at the theater Sunday night."

Margarite shook her head impatiently. "No, I didn't see anyone but Ben." She thrust her chin up. "Ben's not getting away with murder. Detective Bystrom has another witness who saw him on Sunday night."

"Did you see this person?"

Margarite turned coy. "No, I told you. I only saw Ben."

"Do they have a name?"

"Detective Bystrom told me not to talk about him."

So, the other witness was a man who most likely owned the sheepskin coat. Quinn got up and headed for the door. "If you think of anything else, let me know." She turned around with her hand on the doorknob. "You know, I wouldn't be in a big hurry to pick a name for the baby. The doctor commented on Paul's vasectomy in the autopsy notes." She walked out the door, enjoying the sight of Margarite, red-faced and, for once, speechless.

****

Quinn was two miles from her exit to the office when traffic ground to a halt. Up ahead, she saw the police working a multi-car accident. No one was going anywhere until the wrecked vehicles were towed. She sipped coffee from her to-go cup and waited, thinking of what Margarite told Bystrom.

Bystrom had two witnesses who would testify they saw Ben. Margarite would be easy to discredit. She claimed she was pregnant by Paul, who was shooting blanks, and that Ben's bar was losing money, which it wasn't.

Unless it was as busy as a bus stop behind the theater on a freezing cold night, the other witness had to be the person who owned the coat. He and the nameless woman saw each other. All Quinn had to do was find one of them and get them to talk.

The last tow truck rumbled off, and she turned toward the Microtel to talk with Alice. Since she stayed in the camp, she might recognize the woman or the distinctive coat. Three days had passed since Paul's body was found, and she needed a break in the case. Maybe Alice was the key.

Chapter 18

Quinn drove through a fast-food place and bought a bucket of fried chicken, a mountain of fries, and two large sodas. It was midafternoon, and Alice and Sarah had probably already eaten lunch, but Alice could use the extra calories. Quinn wanted the old woman well-fed and happy when she asked if she knew the unknown woman or could identify the owner of the distinctive coat.

The Microtel was in a quiet business section off Thornton Avenue. Sarah answered the door and smiled when she saw the chicken. "Alice does love her fried chicken."

Alice peeked around Sarah and smiled. She wore jeans and a pale pink sweatshirt. Thanks to a trip to a salon at Meadows' expense, Alice's silver hair was clean and freshly cut with soft layers around her face. Her nails were rounded and polished pink. Alice could have passed as someone's sweet grandma.

The room was so small that Quinn and Sarah sat on the beds and watched Alice dig into the food. "Is that guy I saw at the theater in jail yet?" Alice asked in between bites of chicken. "I'd feel a whole lot safer knowing he's behind bars."

"He's not the killer. The murder happened before you got to the theater. The man you saw was screaming because he found his brother's body."

"You mean I went to sleep in there with a dead man

down the hall?"

"Yes."

"I don't like the sound of that." Alice's face scrunched into a web of fine worry lines. She wiped her mouth and fingers on a napkin. "It's bad luck to be nearby when the spirit passes on."

"I'm sorry that happened to you but I need your help. Would you take a look at these pictures?" Quinn handed Alice the picture of the woman wearing the sheepskin coat. "Do you know this person?"

Alice finished eating a chicken leg and put it on a plate. She held the photo close to her nose and squinted. "That's Ray Metchum's coat. What's she doing with it? Ray's mighty proud of that coat. He won it in a poker game and wouldn't give it to anyone. She musta stole it."

Quinn's heart rate kicked up. "Do you know Mr. Metchum?"

"Sure do. He stays in the camp. He's an okay guy, but he can be a cranky old fart when he's been drinking, which is most of the time. You better hope he's sober when you show him that picture because he's going to be mad."

"Does he hang out anywhere else?"

"He goes over to Saint Elizabeth's. They got a nice soup kitchen, and a bunch of us eat there. He used to go to the AA meetings over there with my husband. He had problems with the bottle, too, but I don't know for sure if Ray still goes to those meetings. You know how alcoholics are. All gung-ho one day and sneaking a drink the next."

"Thank you, that's a big help. When you left the theater, did you see anyone?"

Alice shook her head vigorously. "I didn't see

anyone out in that storm. I barely made it to the camp."

"Have you ever seen the woman?"

"Nope. Never saw her before." Alice tucked the lid on the chicken bucket. "Are you going to make me leave now that I've answered your questions?" Her watery blue eyes teared up. "I want to stay put."

What could Quinn promise? Meadows wasn't about to put her up in a hotel indefinitely. Alice would end up back on the streets unless Quinn helped her. "I have a friend who might be able to find you a place to live." Quinn regretted it as soon as she said it. She shouldn't have offered hope when she wasn't sure she could deliver. Alice's life had been hard enough without getting her hopes up, only to let her down. "I'll do my best," she told Alice.

Quinn left the hotel, wishing she had a car that started remotely and would be warm when she slid inside. Last night's storm had raced out of Denver to torment Kansas, leaving behind a numbing, subzero wind chill.

She sat in the motel parking lot, warming her hands over a vent, and called a social worker she'd worked with before. If anyone could help Alice get into a subsidized apartment, he could. When he answered, Quinn explained Alice's predicament. He agreed to visit Alice and thought she would qualify for a Housing Authority voucher.

Quinn texted Sarah that a social worker would be coming by to visit Alice. Before she drove away, she texted Ben and told him she was coming to pick him up. He replied he'd be waiting outside the bar. Quinn headed to the Starlight Lounge, thinking she had only a handful of suppositions until she talked to Ray Metchum or the unknown woman.

Her phone rang as she idled at a stoplight. It was Meadows, and since he rarely called, preferring text or email, Quinn braced herself for the bad news. "The police lab results are back. The blood trail in the Green Room isn't Paul's. They'll want a blood sample from Ben now."

It was the news Quinn suspected would come, but hearing it was still a gut punch. Especially now that there might be two witnesses who would testify Ben was at the scene. "Are the results back from the Bharat lab?"

"No, so it's not doomsday yet. If it is Ben's blood, he'll need to consider a plea deal."

"Does Ben know?"

"I called him first. I didn't mention the plea deal. There will be enough time for that later. "Did you talk to Margarite again?"

Quinn told him about Margarite changing her story. That she'd been at the theater, claimed she saw Ben, and there might be a second witness. "There's a chance the unidentified woman and the person she got the coat from live in the homeless camp. I'm on my way to pick up Ben, and we'll head that way."

****

By the time Quinn pulled in front of the Starlight, the late afternoon gloom had leached the color from the city. Ben was pacing the sidewalk, dressed in a heavy coat and a hat.

A blast of frigid air accompanied him as he got in the car. "Meadows already told me about the blood. You don't have to worry. It's not mine." He fastened his seat belt and turned to Quinn. "What did you find out?"

"The sheepskin coat belongs to Ray Metchum. Alice

knows him from the camp."

"Did she recognize the woman in the photo? Because I didn't find anyone who knew her."

"No such luck," Quinn said.

"Did you talk to Margarite?"

"Yeah, Bystrom had been by to talk to her again. Margarite told him she was so grief-stricken over losing her baby's father that she didn't remember any details until the shock wore off. She told Bystrom she saw you."

Ben's head shot back in surprise. "Is Bystrom buying it?"

"Margarite thinks he believes her. She claims you killed Paul because he wouldn't give you money to bail out the bar."

Ben's voice was tight with fury. "I didn't need Paul's money. My accountant keeps meticulous records, and I'll provide the financial documents to whoever wants to see them."

"Including the statements from your offshore account?"

Ben whipped around to look at her. "If you want to see my statements from the Cayman account, I'd be happy to show them to you."

"If you used one of your multiple identities to make the money, it could be a problem."

He looked taken aback. "At one time, those were important to me. I made a mistake by not destroying them. I will."

Hoping for more, Quinn waited. She desperately wanted to hear him say he was a spy, worked for the DEA or Homeland Security, anything that legitimized the documents and hidden cash. Ben didn't offer any further explanation. "Get rid of them today," she said. "If

163

Bystrom arrests you, he'll get a warrant and search your house."

"You're right, of course. Consider it done."

"Were you at the theater earlier on Sunday night?" Quinn asked.

"No, I wasn't, and Margarite is an unreliable witness. You know that."

Quinn looked over at Ben. "I had to ask."

He nodded. "Asked and answered. "Any other bombshells from Margarite?"

"Bystrom has a second witness who can place you there. My guess is it's a Ray Metchum."

"Then, it will be interesting to see if Mr. Metchum recognizes me," Ben said grimly.

****

Once Quinn and Ben crossed the stone boundary wall between the college and the woods, the tall pines blocked the city lights. Quinn cast a wary eye around her, looking for anyone watching them from the tree line. They were no more than thirty feet into the woods when she smelled wood smoke.

The camp sat in a clearing, less than a ten-minute walk from the college. The unknown woman could have easily walked to the camp and back in the time she was missing from the surveillance video. She might be innocent, have met Metchum, borrowed his coat, twisted her ankle, and limped back to campus.

Except Alice said Metchum would never give his coat away.

The camp was tidy, with a wide path bisecting the center. Fallen trees had been dragged alongside the trail to serve as benches. Sagging old tents, rain-proofed with plastic sheets, sat haphazardly under the few trees.

Grocery baskets, roller bags, camp stoves, and even an old recliner were scattered around. No one was outside in the bitter cold.

"Do we yell hello or what?" Quinn asked.

"I don't know, but I don't want to sneak up on anyone and surprise them," Ben said.

The camp dogs took the decision out of their hands. They came loping toward them, barking their heads off. Quinn and Ben stood still as the ruckus-raising dogs milled around them, and a bearded man wearing a tan jacket over a black shirt and faded jeans came out of a tent. He was so wizened that his Broncos cap slipped over his ears, but he held himself erect.

When he was close, he yelled at the dogs to be quiet. They sat quietly, heads cocked, eyes on him. "I'm Clyde Beeker, the mayor of this town. What do you want?"

A woman with a puppy cradled in the crook of her arm joined him. "Social workers or church people," she said to Clyde. "Got to be one or the other."

"I'm Quinn, and this is my friend, Ben. We're looking for this woman." She held out the picture of the woman wearing Metchum's coat. Quinn wanted to see a reaction to the coat or a hint of recognition of the woman. "She's not in any trouble. We just want to talk to her."

Clyde didn't glance at the photograph. He kept his eyes on her. "Does this have anything to do with the murdered man over at the school? You get the hell out of here if it does. We don't get involved in things that are none of our business."

By now, several people had come out of their shelters. They gathered around Clyde, eyeing Quinn and Ben with distrust. Quinn felt like she had walked through the looking glass and discovered a new tribe. She was talking to a self-styled mayor about his people no more than a short walk from a college campus in a large urban setting.

"We're not with the police and don't want any trouble," Quinn said.

Clyde finally looked at the picture. "What's going on here?" he demanded. "That's not her coat." The group crowded in to see the picture. "That's Metchum's coat,"

"Is Mr. Metchum here?" Ben asked.

Clyde handed Quinn the picture. "We're done here."

"We'd like to talk to him," Quinn said. "There won't be any trouble."

"You got no reason to be up in Metchum's business."

"What do you want to know?" a deep voice asked from the crowd.

Quinn whirled around and saw a meaty six-foot-tall man with a ragged blanket slung around his shoulders.

Clyde thrust the picture at him. "Metchum, look at this."

Metchum glanced at it, then up at Quinn. Then, his gaze lingered on Ben.

Ben pulled his hat off and the scarf down from his face.

Quinn watched Metchum for any sign of recognition. There was none, and Metchum abruptly turned away. "Wait," Quinn called out to him. "Can you help us find her?"

"I don't know anything about her," he said over his shoulder.

"Did you give her the coat?"

"Yeah, sure."

"What's her name?"

166

He did a half-turn and shrugged. "I don't know. She was cold, is all."

"Can you tell me anything about her?"

"Not a thing."

"Wait a minute," Ben said.

Clyde threw his arm out to stop Ben from approaching Metchum.

"Here." Ben peeled off his long down coat and tossed it to Metchum. "Take this."

Metchum dropped the blanket and slipped on the coat. "Thanks, man."

"Go on now," Clyde said to Quinn and Ben.

When they were out of earshot, Quinn turned around and saw Clyde standing with his hands on his hips, watching them. "Metchum didn't recognize you," she said.

Ben brushed the snow off his shoulders. "I noticed, but he's not telling us everything he knows. He didn't give his coat away. His life depends on staying warm."

"I'll track him down tomorrow."

"I'm going with you."

"No, it's no good for him to see you again. He smelled like a brewery, and I don't want him to be confused about when and where he saw you."

Chapter 19

It was late when Quinn dropped Ben at the Starlight and headed home. A sliver of moonlight peeked from behind the clouds, but the holiday lights stole the show. Even though Christmas was less than two weeks away, she didn't have the heart to drag out decorations. She wasn't feeling any joy. She and Charley would be in an apartment by the time Christmas day rolled around. She wondered what the holiday would be like with Ben and envisioned a brightly lit tree with presents and a festive dinner. Then, she reined herself back into reality. It would never happen.

Women like her didn't end up with men like Ben.

Quinn had fed Charley and was on her way to shower when Truck called. "Babe," he said, "I got the information on that gun Bystrom took from your house. It's the murder weapon. My sources tell me the gun mysteriously appeared in the evidence locker, wiped clean of prints."

Quinn wasn't surprised. Bystrom was up to his old tricks. She hoped Trixie would find enough evidence to shut him down. The sooner he was gone, the better.

Truck wasn't finished reporting. "I have that information on Ben Loughty you wanted. It's in your email. You're going to find it interesting. Pull it up, and I'll talk you through it."

Quinn grabbed her laptop and opened her email.

"What am I looking at?"

"Ben Loughty's bank account in the Caymans with a balance of six point eight million dollars."

Stunned, she sat back, kicking herself. She should have called Ben's bluff and had him show her his bank statements.

"He was a successful cat burglar in his former life," Truck said.

Quinn's heart was pounding like a bass drum. "That can't be true."

Truck laughed. "It is. I talked to a retired cop friend of mine on the East Coast. He told me the whole story. The cops think Ben's cellmate taught him the business before he died. Have you ever heard of Ernest Druckheimer? He was a famous cat burglar in Europe before he moved here. He was Ben's cellmate."

Quinn couldn't believe what she was hearing. Ben, a cat burglar? Would she ever peel away all his layers, and if she did, would she like what she found?

"This Druckheimer guy started stealing in Munich back in the eighties. When Western Europe got too hot for him, he moved to the States. Ernest was so slick he could pick through the wife's jewelry while the owner was sleeping in the same room. He operated up and down the East Coast, from Miami to Cape Cod, and stole millions of dollars worth of jewels. He never hurt a soul, and the media dubbed him Superthief. He didn't go to prison for theft. The IRS nailed him on tax fraud. The Feds took his multi-million-dollar mansion in upstate New York and a yacht, but they never found his cash. That's where your client comes into the story.

"Ernest died of pancreatic cancer a few months before Ben got out of the joint," Truck continued. "A year after Ben was released, he bought and restored a nineteenth-century home in Baltimore. Six months later, a summer home in The Hamptons was robbed. Then, like clockwork, there were thefts from the tip of Florida to Maine with an occasional heist in Europe."

The hits kept coming. Could it be a mistake? Just because Ben shared a cell with a famous thief didn't mean he became one himself. "It's a heck of a good story, but I need more than that to believe he's guilty of a string of B and E's."

"Have I ever let you down?" he asked. "Look at the spreadsheet."

Quinn opened the attachment.

"Look down the first column," he advised. "Those are the dates of each robbery. Now, look at the second column. That's the date Ben deposited money into his offshore account."

Quinn scanned the two columns and sucked in a breath. Months after each robbery, Ben deposited money into his account.

"He only made deposits after heists," Truck said. "The last burglary was over four years ago, and you know what? Superthief's old fence died about the same time the thefts ended, and Ben moved to Denver. It all fits, Babe. Your client is a retired cat burglar. Picked up where Ernest left off and used the same fence."

Quinn double-checked the columns, praying Truck was wrong, but he wasn't. "What are these regular withdrawals titled *CC*?"

"The *CC* stands for Catholic Charities. I did some checking. The donations were made after a natural disaster. He donated after the hurricane in Haiti and to Ethiopia during the famine. The last contribution was to a Ukrainian Relief fund. Looks like your guy fashioned himself as a modern-day Robin Hood. There was nearly ten million in the account at one time, but he's in no danger of going broke. He's invested in a portfolio of blue-chip stocks and is making money hand over fist."

Quinn was dumbfounded. She'd fantasized about having a relationship with a man who was an international jewel thief. How crazy was that?

"What are you going to do now about your client?"

Good question.

"Do what you need to, Quinn. Call me if you need me."

Quinn glanced at the clock. The bar was still open, and she bet Ben was there. She texted him she was on her way, then drove like a crazy woman. What was wrong with her that she picked men who were either unavailable or the wrong sort? Ben was a thief. The passports, credit cards, hidden cash, and Truck's spreadsheet painted a compelling picture.

She turned east on Colfax, crossed the interstate, sped past the light rail station on the Front Range campus, and only slowed down when she saw the Golden Dome of the Capitol. She was running on anger. Ben had shared only the best tidbits of his life, like someone on a social media site creating a fantasy life. Yeah, he'd been in Amsterdam, Berlin, and London, only he was stealing jewelry, not buying stones for clients.

Quinn understood the part that chance played in peoples' lives. If her parents hadn't abandoned her to be raised by her grandparents, she wouldn't be who she is. It was chance that put Ben in a cell with a master thief who taught him a skill and left him a fortune. But it was by choice that Ben followed in Superthief's footsteps.

Ben didn't have to become a jewel thief. He *wanted* to be a thief.

When she strode into the bar, she was still fuming and certain she looked like a woman who could chew nails and spit out nickels.

Ben sought her out and steered her through the crowd. "Do you want something to drink?"

"No, thank you. Let's go to your office." Quinn led the way, and neither spoke as they walked to the back of the bar.

She sat in one of the metal chairs while Ben perched on his desk, looking down at her. "What's this about?" he asked.

"You were a jewel thief."

His eyes widened in surprise. "I was."

Quinn's heart thundered in her ears, and she was battling a storm of emotions.

He raised both hands, palms out. "Please, stay and listen. Then, if you want to leave, I won't ask anything of you."

She sat back and folded her arms across her chest. "Go ahead. Let's hear it."

"When I was eighteen and got arrested, I was a cocky little shit. My Dad did all he could to help me, hired a great lawyer, paid my legal fees, and after I was sentenced, he hired an ex-con to teach me how to survive in prison. I still acted like an ungrateful fool. Then, the cell door clanged behind me, and I nearly lost it. I looked at the men around me and was terrified. If my cellie hadn't protected me, I would have died within a week."

Ben stood, stretched the tension out of his neck and shoulders, went over to the bookshelf, and straightened a picture.

172

Quinn stayed quiet. She wanted to hear what he had to say before she said her mind.

He turned around and remained standing. "I'm not proud of what I'm telling you."

"Go ahead, please."

Ben sat beside her. "My cellmate was Ernest Druckheimer, the famous jewel thief turned celebrity. He robbed the poshest homes in Europe and America, lived like a king, and partied on the Riviera. The royalty of Europe partied with him, never knowing he was eyeing their jewels."

Quinn had to lean forward to hear him. The music thundered through the walls, and the crowd sang at the top of their voices.

"I'm sorry. It's the bar's first karaoke night. Would you like to go someplace quieter to talk?"

"No, here's fine."

Ben raked his hand through his hair and took a deep breath. "Ernest took me under his wing and tutored me in the art of becoming a mini-him. Then, he was diagnosed with a fast-moving cancer. I was terrified of what would happen to me after he died, but the gangs left me alone. It was like I'd inherited Ernest's celebrity status. On the morning I was released, Paul picked me up and took me to my parents' house. I was an angry ex-con who thought nothing was my fault. I was at loose ends. I applied for jobs, but as it turned out, an ex-con with a GED certificate isn't qualified to do much. Within a month of my release, a lawyer contacted me and told me he had a letter for me from Ernest. I walked into his office, and he handed me a handwritten letter dated three months before Ernest died. The letter directed me to return to the lawyer's office precisely one year after receiving it. Until then, I wasn't to contact the attorney or tell anyone about the letter.

"The lawyer wouldn't answer any of my questions. He just kept saying, 'Return one year from today.' I left his office angrier than when I arrived. I felt tooled around from beyond the grave. I took to prowling the streets at night, sleeping all day, and snapping at my family. I looked up old friends, but I didn't know them anymore. They were in college, had steady girlfriends, and were excited about their job prospects. I couldn't get any traction. I was on a one-year leash and couldn't figure out what to do with myself. Finally, Dad got fed up and said I couldn't stay at home. He hoped it would jar loose whatever kept me from getting on with my life. I hitchhiked around the country, working as a day laborer and often sleeping rough until the year had passed. When I returned to Ernest's lawyer, he handed me a bank statement from an account in the Cayman Islands with millions of dollars and my name on it. I decided to pick up where Ernest left off.

"My Dad paid for my courses to earn a gemologist credential. He was thrilled I'd found a purpose. No one knew what I was really up to. When I finished my training, a friend of Dad's knew someone who knew someone, and on their recommendation, De Beers hired me as a diamond appraiser. I moved to Baltimore and was soon buying jewels for the uber-wealthy. I was invited into their homes, and I got to know them. I saw how they lived and where they kept their treasures. One night, I faxed my resignation to De Beers, and within a week, I robbed my first house." Ben had a death grip on the edge of the desk. "I chose to be a thief. I was an adrenaline junkie. I got a high when I sneaked into a mark's house and walked out with his wife's jewelry. Like Ernest, I believed in the romantic notion of taking from the rich and giving to the poor. I tried to convince myself that donating money absolved me from stealing. I was wrong."

The music ended, and there were the sounds of furniture scooting across the floor and the murmur of voices as the crowd left. Ben looked up from the floor at her. "I'm sorry, this isn't the best place to have this conversation."

Quinn's heart and head battled for her attention. Her heart believed Ben had changed. He was honest about his past and owned his mistakes. Her head was having a more challenging time accepting him, but who was she to judge him? She wasn't the same woman she had once been.

"Everything changed for me when my Dad died of a heart attack," Ben said softly. I hadn't gone home in years or been a good son, and the time had passed for me to tell him I loved him. I knew Dad would be ashamed of me if he knew what I became. I could never make it up to him, but I decided to turn my life around and become the man my dad would have been proud of. I came home to be here for Mom and Paul.

"I told Paul everything. He promised to help me start over and was with me every step of the way, but it hasn't been easy. My old life was exciting. From the moment I started planning the heist until I held the stone in my hand, I was living on the edge of danger. I can't tell you how alive I felt. Walking away from my old life was like kicking an addiction."

Ben sat up straight and looked Quinn in the eye. "I'm not the man I was. I had an opportunity to return to

175

my old life and didn't take it. Three months ago, an old client contacted me about a job. He wanted me to steal a two hundred and fifteen-million-dollar diamond cut from the Cullinan, the famous stone found a hundred years ago in South Africa. Stealing a stone cut from the Cullinan would have been the biggest heist of my life. He offered me a twenty-five percent finder's fee. All I had to do was steal it from a display case in a resort in Los Angeles.

"I didn't take the job. I've turned my back on all I was and become the man I should have been long ago. I know good acts don't wash away the bad. I'll never make things right, and I can't promise I'll ever be a perfect man, but I *am* a changed man." Ben leaned over and put his hand on hers. "I care what you think of me. More than you can imagine." His voice was husky. "I think you have feelings, too, and I don't want to lose what we might have. Give me a chance."

Quinn felt light-headed. She thought she was in love with him. "I know something about how hard it is to change. I'm not the woman who watched her lover shot to death by his wife. I've carried that guilt every day since it happened."

She saw the look of astonishment flit across his face and knew she might never tell him if she stopped. "David was an assistant D.A., ten years older than me, handsome and experienced, and going places. I was an intern. Every time we saw each other, the air sizzled. I was afraid everyone in the office could see we were hot for each other. I knew he was married. He had a picture of his wife and two daughters on his desk, but I was secretly thrilled when he asked me out. Though, I knew I wouldn't go. I told him I didn't go out with married men, and he said he understood. Things went back to normal. It was like he'd never approached me. Then, I was assigned to work for him. He was prosecuting a big case and under a lot of pressure to win. As the trial date got closer, we worked nights and weekends. I could tell he was still into me. One evening, it was late, and he had dinner sent in. Everyone else had gone home. Just the two of us were in the conference room. David told me that he had loved me since we met. He said he and his wife were legally separated and that he'd moved into an apartment. That their divorce was something they both wanted, and they had worked out the custody arrangement for the girls. He said all the right things, and I'm ashamed of how happy I was that he was available. I believed him. I'd been in love with him for a long time and thought we had a chance to build a life together. Even though the divorce wasn't final, I began to spend the night with him in his apartment."

Holding up one hand, Ben said gently, "Quinn, you don't have to tell me all this. It won't change how I feel about you."

"I want you to know who I was," Quinn said quietly.

"I understand." Ben took her hand in his.

"One night, we ordered Chinese food. I was setting the table when I heard the knock on the door. David said he would get it, and when he opened the door, he cried out his wife's name. I looked up in time to see her shoot him and bolt down the hall. I ran to David and put my hand on his chest to try and stop the bleeding, but he was already dead. I sat by him until the police arrived. They took me to the station to make a statement and released me early the following morning. After his wife was arrested, I discovered everything David had told me was a lie. There was no petition for divorce. He was living at home and using the apartment to see me, telling his wife he was sleeping in his office. His wife had become suspicious and followed him that night. Their girls had just turned four and six when their mother went to prison. Her parents took the girls. The children lost their home, their dad, and their mother. I've never forgiven myself."

Ben tucked her hair behind her ears. His hand lingered on her cheek. "I think you've beaten yourself up long enough over the affair. You can't judge your younger self for not having the wisdom you have now. It's not fair to you." He kissed her gently. "We've both made mistakes, and there's nothing we can't face together. Let me drive you home."

"Thank you, but I'm okay with driving. I should go now." Quinn knew if he took her home, she would take him to her bed. Now wasn't the time.

When Quinn crawled into bed, she thought about how she and Ben had laid their souls bare and opened themselves to judgment. Neither of them had turned away in disgust. She loved him, but they were different people with little in common, and he was still a client. Where would a homewrecker and an international cat burglar find common ground? She wasn't in his class. Ben knew about art, collected expensive things, traveled the world, and had picked up a touch of Europe in his voice and manners. Her East Denver roots would matter to a man like him.

Chapter 20

Quinn woke on Thursday morning in a rush to get to St. Elizabeth's Church before they finished serving breakfast. Metchum could be the linchpin she needed to break this case.

She headed north on Federal and took Colfax to Eleventh Street to the Romanesque nineteenth-century building. The church was adjacent to a light rail station and a bus stop, providing easy access to hot meals and showers for those in need. By the time she'd parked at the church, Ben had texted, asking her to call him after she talked to Metchum.

The queue for breakfast wound out the basement door and through the meditation garden. There was some grumbling and a couple of glares as Quinn edged to the front of the line. She saw Ben's down coat draped over a chair in the back of the room where Metchum sat alone. He was hunched over a plate of bacon and eggs, sopping up the yolks with a thick piece of toast. She took the chair across from him.

Metchum stopped eating and looked up at her. He jabbed at her with a piece of toast. "I don't want to talk to you."

"Good morning, Mr. Metchum," Quinn said as she sat across from him. "I think you know more about what happened on Sunday night than you've told me."

"I didn't kill anybody."

"I don't believe you did. What are you scared of?"

He shrugged and tucked into his breakfast. "Nothing. This isn't none of my business. Stay away from me. I got enough trouble."

"Who is giving you trouble?"

He scooted back his chair and reached for his coat.

Quinn pulled out a business card and folded a twenty-dollar bill around it. "If you want to talk, call me."

Metchum snatched the money and tucked it into his pocket, but her card fluttered to the floor as he hurried out the side door.

Quinn followed him as he cut across Tenth Street. She raced after him before the light changed and trailed behind him on the opposite side of the street. He looked over his shoulder once, and Quinn turned toward a shop window. From the reflection in the window glass, she saw him keep walking. He picked up his pace when they were a block from a light rail station. He elbowed his way to the front of the crowd, waiting to board. Quinn hung back.

The H-line train pulled in, and when the first car's door opened, Metchum jumped on the train and sat on the second bench from the front, looking straight ahead.

Quinn scrambled to get on the next car and managed to squeeze in before the door whooshed closed. The train was packed, and she had to stand, hanging onto a pole, but she was near the door and could see Metchum when he left the train.

The light rail barreled into the first station. Metchum stayed on the train. After two more stops, Metchum got off at the Knox station in a neighborhood of modest frame homes. Quinn mingled with the crowd until

Metchum was off the platform and striding north.

She followed him two blocks to a neighborhood of shabby, small bungalows. Gentrification hadn't reached this far from the high-rise towers of downtown.

Metchum walked up worn steps to a faded brown house with a broken porch railing. She stood across the street, mixing with people at a bus stop, and watched Metchum knock on the door.

A teenage boy opened the door and called over his shoulder to someone while blocking Metchum from entering. A frazzled-haired, plump woman came to the door and didn't look happy to see Metchum. She folded her arms across her chest and stood in the doorway. The boy stayed protectively beside her while the woman and Metchum talked.

Quinn wasn't close enough to hear them, but it looked like an unpleasant conversation. The woman threw up both hands like she was exasperated. The boy moved protectively closer to the woman. Suddenly, a small child barreled around the woman, screaming, "Daddy," as she jumped into Metchum's outstretched arms and buried her face in his neck.

The woman pulled the little girl out of his arms, said something to Metchum, and shook her head. The teenage boy blocked Metchum from entering when she backed away, still holding the child. Metchum dug in his pocket, pulled out the money she'd given him, and held it out to the boy. The boy grabbed it and closed the door in Metchum's face. He shuffled down the steps to the street. Once, he paused to look back at the house.

Quinn crossed the street and called, "Metchum."

When he saw her, he wiped the tears from his face and stood straighter.

"You have a nice-looking family," she said as she fell in step with him.

"They were my family. Allie left me and took the kids."

"I'm sorry. Your little girl is adorable," Quinn said.

"She's the light of my life."

"I can see that. Let me buy you a cup of coffee."

He didn't say no, so when she saw a small diner, she stopped and opened the door. "How about this place?" He nodded, and she steered him past a handful of customers to the back of the restaurant.

Quinn ordered the special for Metchum since she'd chased him away from his free breakfast. She waited until the waitress had poured his second cup of coffee and he'd cleaned his plate before she showed him the picture of the nameless woman wearing his coat. "You were behind the theater Sunday night. What happened?"

Metchum looked sad and defeated. "I never saw that woman before Sunday night, and that's God's truth. I was drunk out of my mind. I tried to get into the theater to sleep it off and must have passed out by the door. I came to when she was rolling me over and stealing my coat. I guess she got my hat, too. I don't remember, but it's gone. The cops found me sleeping it off in the woods the next morning. A detective told me a man got killed in the theater and asked if I'd seen anyone. I told them about the woman taking my coat, but he kept asking who else I saw. I told them I was drunk and didn't remember seeing anyone but her. I don't want anything more to do with this. Don't come around me again. I don't know any of you people, and I don't want to."

"Who was the detective?"

Metchum stirred his coffee, sloshing it on the table.

"Bystrom," he answered.

"Tell me what's going on," Quinn said.

"I can't. My boy is in enough trouble."

"What kind of trouble?"

"You can't help my son."

"I work for a law firm. We might be able to help you if you tell me what the trouble is."

Metchum's shoulders slumped. "My boy and a bunch of kids robbed a convenience store. The owner pulled a shotgun from behind the counter, and one of the boys tackled him before he could get a shot off. The old guy hit his head and died. My boy is charged with murder. He swore to me that he didn't push the old man."

"What does Detective Bystrom want from you in return for dropping the murder charge?"

Metchum shook his head. "Not talking to you."

"My boss is a good lawyer."

"He can't help us. Bystrom told me he'd see to it my boy got the death penalty if I didn't swear that guy you were with at the camp was at the theater on Sunday night. It's a done deal. My boy's not going to die."

"I didn't realize you recognized him. He didn't kill his brother, and you could get into trouble. It's a crime to give false information to the police."

Metchum shrugged. "Then, I'm damned if I do and damned if I don't."

He scooted his chair back and stalked out of the diner.

Quinn walked out behind Metchum, texting Ben that she was headed his way.

She was only minutes from meeting Ben at the Starlight when her phone alerted her to an email from Molly Bresson. She pulled to the curb, curious about what her source in the police wanted. A desk officer at the Midtown Denver PD Station, Molly was a single mom with money problems, a sharp mind, and a tongue to match. She didn't mind looking out for herself and her kid by peddling information she skived from confidential police files.

A video file was attached to the email along with a message. *I thought this might be worth some money to you.* The time icon indicated the video was fifteen seconds long. Quinn tapped play, and the video opened on a shot of the stage door of the Alderberry Theater, time-stamped with Sunday's date and 7:44 p.m. Two seconds into the film, Ben walked out of the theater. Quinn's gut tightened. Two eyewitnesses and a video placing him at the murder scene would put him in prison.

Except… something was wrong. Quinn clearly recalled from the surveillance video shot on Sunday night that the temperature had plummeted to below zero and heavy snow had fallen.

Yet Ben was hatless and wearing only a long-sleeved shirt and a down vest.

It didn't make any sense unless . . . the video was faked. Someone had inserted Sunday's date and time over a video clip of Ben visiting Paul on a different evening. Was Deke Bystrom so desperate to make an arrest that he fabricated evidence to lend credibility to Margarite and Metchum's stories?

She was so angry that she angled parked across two parking spots behind the Starlight. She saw the lights of Ben's car approaching. Just as he parked in the slot next to Quinn, two cop cars sped into the alley, sirens blaring, lights flashing, followed by a dark sedan. The cop cars had blocked both exits by the time Deke Bystrom and a uniformed patrolman got out of the sedan and walked toward Ben.

Quinn jumped out of her car. "What's going on?"

Detective Bystrom ignored her. "Mr. Loughty, I'm arresting you for the murder of Paul Loughty."

A cop brought Ben's arms around his back.

"On what evidence?" Quinn asked.

"Ms. Kane. A pleasure to see you," Bystrom said as the officer cuffed Ben. "Your client's blood is at the scene of the crime."

Quinn tried to hide her shock. She told Ben, "Mr. Meadows will meet us at the station." As the two cop cars left with Ben in custody, she called her boss. Martha answered his cell phone and said Meadows was in a conference with an opposing attorney, negotiating a settlement.

"He'll take my call. Interrupt the meeting."

Then, Meadows was on the line. She told him Ben had been arrested, and the blood at the scene was their client's.

"I'm on my way," he said, and the line was dead.

Quinn called Doc Iverson, hoping he'd finished his blood analysis at the crime scene. When he didn't answer her call, she left him a message to call her as soon as possible.

She arrived at the station before Meadows and waited for him in her car. They'd need a few minutes alone for her to get him up to speed.

Fifteen minutes later, Meadows squeezed his bulk into the front passenger seat.

"Are the results back from the Bharat Lab?" she asked, not giving him time to speak.

"Not yet. Did you find the second witness?"

Quinn nodded. "Bystrom is bribing Ray Metchum to say he saw Ben at the theater. His son is charged with murder, and Bystrom threatened he'd make sure the boy got the death penalty if Metchum didn't stick to the story. He'll lie to save his son."

Meadows smiled a wintry smile. "Coercing Metchum to provide false testimony is a crime. I'll chat with the District Attorney and tell him Metchum is under duress from Bystrom. Did Metchum identify the unknown woman?"

"No, he's either protecting her or doesn't know who she is." Quinn passed Meadows her phone, cued to the video. "I received this a few minutes ago. It's a fake."

Meadows kneaded the bridge of his nose. "Do you have the camera or the memory card?"

She shook her head and pointed to the screen. "You can tell by the angle of the shot that this camera wasn't on the college's property. It was mounted in the woods on city property. Someone was spying on the theater."

"It was probably Paul. He was obsessed with the lack of security," Meadows said. "He asked if I thought he'd get caught putting a camera up on city property. I advised him not to. He'd feel terrible if he knew Bystrom was trying to convict his brother with footage from a camera he set, but anyone can see it's fake. The D.A. wouldn't put this in front of a judge for fear he would be laughed out of the courthouse."

Meadows opened the car door. "I have to meet with Ben." He looked over his shoulder at Quinn. "The facial recognition program you wanted is at the office. I'm damned tired of hearing about that unknown woman. Find out who she is."

Quinn had scarcely pulled away from the curb when

Trixie called. "Hey, you're in your car. Can you talk?"

"Ben's been arrested. His blood matches the blood at the crime scene."

"Oh, wow, I didn't see that coming. Where is he?"

"At the Midtown Station. Meadows is with him." Quinn sped up and flew through a yellow light.

"Do you want to call me back?" Trixie asked.

"No. Have you found anything on Bystrom?"

"Bystrom's on the take."

Quinn could hear the glee in Trixie's voice.

"It was ridiculously easy to find," Trixie said. "He must have thought making the rank of detective made him the Teflon Kid."

Quinn saw an oncoming car swerve across the center line and head straight toward her. She yanked the wheel to the right and cut into a stream of traffic. Her phone tumbled to the floorboard, and she heard Trixie's tinny voice, "Hello? Quinn, are you still there?"

The oncoming car veered back into his lane, and behind Quinn came the angry squeal of brakes and horns honking. A truck rolled within inches of her car, and the air brakes hissed so loud she couldn't hear what Trixie was saying. Quinn saw a pull-out ahead, turned off, and parked. She was shaking like a leaf when she grabbed the phone. "Some idiot crossed the center line and nearly hit me head-on."

"Are you okay?"

"Yeah, I'm fine, except I'm about to jump out of my skin. Tell me about Bystrom."

"Bystrom laundered money through the dress store accounts."

"How much money are we talking about?"

"Nine thousand nine hundred and ninety-nine

dollars monthly," Trixie said. "One dollar less than the amount the sending bank has to report to the federal government. The Bystroms never paid a penny of income tax on it."

"Nice, as long as you can get away with it. What bank sent the money?" Quinn asked.

"Grand Summit Bank," Trixie said. "Latham's in it up to his neck. This is tax evasion on a large scale. I faxed what I found to an FBI agent in the local office who works in the organized crime division. He will be so far up both their asses that he can see what they ate for breakfast."

Quinn hadn't realized she was clenching the steering wheel so tightly until she pried her aching fingers off. Trixie had nailed Bystrom and tied him to Latham, but it didn't solve Ben's problem. He was charged with murder.

****

Quinn returned to the office determined to find the identity of the unknown woman. Meadows wasn't the only one tired of the woman being nameless, though identifying her wouldn't be easy. Facial recognition software had bugs. One readily available commercial package had identified a well-known female of color as a white male. The most successful searches had narrow search terms, and Quinn had been compiling a list in her head.

While the software loaded, Quinn checked the properties of the photo of the woman from the surveillance footage. The resolution was low because it was shot at night with a cheap camera, and it didn't help that the woman wore a hat that cast shadows over her face. Quinn used a photography software program to lighten the shadows. With the addition of a sharpener filter, the photo was much clearer. Quinn enlarged the picture and looked at the girl's bone structure. She had a rounded eye orbit, large eyes, a broad face with prominent cheekbones, and a pronounced jawline. Quinn thought she might be part Native American but couldn't be sure. If the girl was a Native American, finding a match would be more difficult. Facial recognition algorithms were biased against identifying females and people of color. The error rate for women of color was over thirty percent, a much higher error rate than for white males.

She picked up the phone and called an old professor of hers in the Anthropology department at her alma mater. She was the go-to expert in forensic facial recognition and worked with the police when they found skeletal remains. Quinn had turned to her before for help. The professor offered to help. Quinn explained what she needed, emailed the photo, and worried her lower lip with her teeth while waiting to hear what the expert said. When the professor called back, she agreed the woman appeared to be part Native American.

Quinn added Native American to the list of search terms and set the software to hunt for a match to the picture. She was confident that if the woman had a state or national ID, her image was in one of the many databases, FBI, Homeland Security, Department of Defense, or local and state law enforcement. Every American was in a virtual police lineup twenty-four hours a day.

While the software searched for a match, Quinn checked her emails and phone messages. Still, no word from Meadows about Ben. She didn't know if that was good news, but the waiting was killing her.

The software signaled a match to a Colorado driver's license issued to Katherine Kendall, and there was a local address near the Denver Arts College. Quinn wondered if the girl had ever attended classes where Paul taught. Quinn knew the college wouldn't confirm or deny if Katherine had attended the school or been employed there because everyone was touchy about violating the privacy laws.

Quinn was a nervous hacker, and it took several exasperating tries before she slipped into the backdoor of the college's website and into the database of students. She found that Katherine had been a student for two semesters and registered as a drama major. She'd been expelled last spring, and noted on the withdrawal was the recension of the Alderberry Scholarship. Katherine had known Paul, and getting expelled and losing a scholarship could make a girl want to murder someone. Finally, Quinn had her break.

She backed out of the college website without leaving digital tracks and searched public records for a police record or property purchases in Katherine's name. She found none. The local address on her license, Jayden Place, might not be current, so Quinn checked the utility company records. The only address associated with Katherine's name was the one on her driver's license. Maybe Katherine hadn't moved. Quinn grabbed her bag and sprinted to her car.

Chapter 21

Quinn texted Katherine's name and her background to her boss. Meadows replied that a disgruntled student who was near the theater and disguised her appearance was no match for a prosecutor with two sworn witness statements and lab results. He texted in all caps. *Find the damn woman.* Like that wasn't what she had been trying to do. She swore she wouldn't contact Meadows again until she had found the girl.

Quinn cruised past the apartment house on Jayden Place, one of several aging buildings popular with the budget-minded college crowd and near the campus. She parked at the end of the block and doubled back on foot. The building's paint was sunbaked beige, and the concrete sidewalks were stained and cracked. Laundry fluttered from the balconies, and bicycles were chained to the railings. There wouldn't be much joy in calling this place home.

The drab foyer had a wall of metal mailboxes and a stained vinyl floor. A paper sign with a hand pointing to the left said, *Manager*.

A middle-aged man answered Quinn's knock. "I don't have any vacancies."

"I'm looking for a friend of mine. Katherine Kendall."

"Never heard of her."

Quinn smiled and stuck her foot between the door

and the frame. "Maybe she left a forwarding address?"

"I can't give out that kind of information."

"I need to—" Quinn said before yelping in pain as the guy rammed the door on her foot. She limped away, hoping to find a talkative tenant.

She struck out when she approached a young man carrying a garbage bag to the chute at the end of the hall. He ignored her and never broke his stride. She had no better luck when she asked a young woman with a backpack stuffed with books.

Quinn took the stairs two at a time and nearly ran into two girls in the hall. She approached them with a big smile and told them she was looking for her cousin. That their great aunt had died and left them each a thousand dollars. Quinn embellished the story by telling the girls the lawyer was ready to write the checks and needed an address for Katherine. "This is the last address any of the family have for her. Does she still live here?"

The shorter girl with spiky dark hair and penetrating chestnut eyes shook her head. She said she'd never heard of anyone named Katherine Kendall.

The taller girl told her friend, "Kat left before you moved in. I remember her. We partied some." She wrinkled her brow. "I don't remember her mentioning any family."

Quinn smiled. "I didn't know I had a great aunt until her lawyer tracked me down and gave me the good news. I bet Kat needs the money as much as I do. Do you know where she moved to?"

"It's over on Irving Street, near the public library. She roped me into helping her move. All I remember is the apartment building is blue."

Quinn was running when the girl called out, "Tell

Kat hi for me."

She was in such a rush she slipped on the ice in front of the building and nearly fell. As she buckled her seat belt, the phone rang. She heard the panic in Sarah's voice. "Alice has had a heart attack. We're at the emergency room at Denver Regional."

"How is she?"

"I'm not family, so I can't find out much, but I don't think it's good. They're taking her up to the ICU in a few minutes. When I brought her in, they asked me for her insurance. I didn't know anything about it, and then one of the clerks said she was old enough to be on Medicare. But I don't know if Alice ever got on it. I can't reach Mr. Meadows."

"He's in court. Call Martha. She'll sort out the insurance. Can you stay with Alice?"

"Yes, of course."

"Great, thank you. Tell Alice she has an apartment waiting for her when she leaves the hospital. Maybe that will give her something to look forward to."

"Thanks, that should cheer her up."

Quinn dropped the phone in the console. If Alice died, Ben wouldn't have an alibi. No one else could testify that Ben arrived after Paul was murdered. By now, Trixie's fax had started a firestorm, but the wheels of justice turned slowly. It could be weeks before Bystrom felt the heat of a federal investigation. It was like the universe was scheming to put Ben in prison.

It was getting late, and Quinn hadn't heard a peep from Meadows. While James Meadows was the best defense attorney in town, it wouldn't be easy to convince a judge to allow Ben out on bail—not with the evidence against Ben and his history as an ex-con. And, if Ben hadn't destroyed the passports and credit cards hidden in his kitchen and the police found them, he'd stay in jail until the trial ended.

Quinn was so preoccupied that she nearly missed the turn onto Irving Street. She made a quick lane change, and the guy driving behind her gave her the finger and honked his horn in protest. She waved at him while she searched both sides of the street until she saw a faded blue apartment house with a vacancy sign stuck out front in a snowbank.

Quinn picked her way across the ice-crusted sidewalk to the front door. The two-story building squatted so close to the street that there wasn't a grass strip between the sidewalk and the road. If the first-floor tenants stuck their arms out the window, they could feel the wind from the cars whizzing by.

The inside hallway was dark, with trash bins overflowing by the stairs and no sign of an onsite manager. Angry voices filtered out of the first apartment she approached. She passed on to another unit and knocked on the door. No one answered, though she heard footsteps inside. She rapped on two more doors, and either no one was home, or they didn't want to talk. It was the kind of building where the tenants looked out the peephole, and if they didn't know you, they played not at home.

Quinn ran down the hallway, knocking on doors, worrying she was wasting time. What if it was only a coincidence Kat was near the theater Sunday night? What if the connection between Metchum and Kat had nothing to do with Paul's murder?

Then, at the end of the hall, she heard a baby crying. The fussing grew louder outside a door left ajar. Quinn poked her head in, and the room looked like a cubicle farm, except the partitions were chain-length fencing. It was a storage room where all the tenants' possessions were locked behind flimsy wire gates and in full view of everyone. There were Christmas trees, old rocking chairs, baby gear, and stacks of dusty boxes. She followed the sounds of the baby's cries and found a tired-looking young woman rooting through a box of baby clothes. The baby sat in a stroller, fretting and kicking his chubby legs.

"Hello, I'm Quinn Kane. I was looking for the manager."

The woman jerked her head up in surprise and pulled the stroller closer to her.

"Sorry, I didn't mean to sneak up on you," Quinn said.

The woman was pretty, with a full mouth and long, curly brown hair. "I'm the manager. Can I help you?"

Quinn pulled out her card. "I'm an investigator with the Meadows law firm. Our client passed away. He and a tenant of yours, Katherine Kendall, knew each other. I wanted to ask her a few questions."

"You mean like he was her boyfriend?"

Quinn smiled. "I don't know that I would call him that."

"Whatever." She shrugged her shoulders. "Kat doesn't live here anymore. I had to evict her for not paying her rent. I'd never had to do that before, and it was the scariest day of my life. She's a creepy chick." She hoisted the fussy child up on her hip and jiggled him. "If you find her, don't tell her I talked to you. I don't want her coming around here."

"I won't tell her a thing. What scared you about

her?"

"She was mad all the time, crazy-like, talking to herself out loud and punching the air."

"I wouldn't want her to live around her either." Quinn commiserated. "Do you know where she went?"

"Yeah, she left an address. I remember it because my mom's second husband moved there when he left us. It's an old house in Five Points on the corner of Emerson and Twenty-fourth Street. It's across the street from a vacant lot and a church." She stroked the baby's hair. "Please, don't tell her I told you where she was. Don't say anything about us."

"I won't, and thanks for the help."

Quinn sprinted to her car. The Five Points neighborhood was on the northeast side of Denver's central business district near Coors Field and Union Station. While it was one of Denver's oldest neighborhoods and one of the fastest growing, gentrification was spotty. The crime rate was nearly twice the Denver average. There were islands where up-and-coming professionals pushed six-hundred-dollar jogging strollers, and a few streets over, the gangs were dealing drugs in the shade of a burned-out building.

Quinn parked on Emerson Street in front of a run-down nineteenth-century two-story house across from the church. The wrap-around porch was littered with mismatched plastic lawn chairs, battered metal folding chairs, and a bright purple bean bag. Empty coffee cans served as ashtrays. She walked through an impressive carved front door with etched glass inserts into an entryway with chipped black and white marble floors. A single bare bulb hung from the ceiling. A sweeping staircase, reminiscent of another time when women in long dresses poised at the top to be viewed before descending, divided the first story into four apartments. Two units on either side of the stairs. No one answered the door in either of the units on the south side. She crossed the foyer and knocked on another door.

No one came to the door, but a stooped older woman opened the door of the adjacent apartment. "No one lives there, dear. Miss Kat's moved."

"I was hoping to talk with her," Quinn said.

The woman's arms begin to shake with the effort of holding herself erect on the walker.

"Let me help you inside," Quinn said, supporting the woman's arm. "My name is Quinn."

"Thank you. I'm Helen Simmons. I hate this getting old. I'm just so unsteady on my feet."

Quinn helped her into her apartment, filled with heavy, dark furniture. Knickknacks covered every flat surface: collections of plates, thimbles, clowns, and sweet-looking smiling children dressed in Swiss clothes. Quinn helped Helen into the only overstuffed chair, upholstered in a chintz rose pattern. A large yellow tabby cat jumped in Helen's lap and purred.

"This is my Morris. He's a sweet boy. Sit down, dear."

Quinn perched on a worn gray sofa. She was anxious to get to the point. "I work for the Meadows law firm. We're settling an estate and need to talk with Ms. Kendall."

"Is Miss Kat in any trouble?"

"Not that I know of. It's routine to talk to the people who know the deceased. Do you know where Kat moved or maybe where she works?"

"No, dear, I never asked her any questions. Young

people don't like nosy neighbors. She is a troubled young woman, and I didn't want to upset her."

"What do you mean by troubled?"

"She wasn't quite right in the head, poor girl. I had a cousin with a girl like Kat, and nothing good came of it. She was the only young person in the building, and we tried to befriend her, but she didn't take to us. Once, I heard her yelling something terrible inside her apartment. I knocked on her door to see if she needed help. I thought something was wrong when she didn't come to the door. The door was unlocked, so I went in and called her name, and she turned on me like a mad dog. I got myself home and locked my door. I'm glad she moved, though I do wish the poor girl well."

Quinn thanked her and left. She'd reached a dead end and failed Ben. She was sitting in her car with the car heater cranked high, beating up on herself when Doc Iverson called. "I have that analysis of the blood trail at the Loughty murder scene."

"Just a moment." Quinn scrambled to dig a pen and paper out of her bag. "Okay, I'm ready."

"The blood trail is from low-velocity spatter. That means it didn't spew from an artery or even a bad cut. It dripped on the floor. All the drops are the same elliptical shape, with the tails extending in the same direction, which means someone walked slowly *out* of the room, dripping blood. There's no indication that anyone came into the room bleeding."

"But Paul didn't fight with his killer. He had no defensive wounds, so how did the killer get wounded inside the room?"

Iverson cut her off. "I do the science; you do the detecting. I have a customer arriving who lost a knife fight, and I don't have any more time to discuss this. That's my opinion, and I stand by it."

Iverson hung up, leaving Quinn to wonder how the killer could be bleeding on the way out of the room but not while entering. As if the blood trail wasn't bizarre enough, why would a murderer slow-walk away from a crime, dripping blood that could be used as evidence against him? Anyone with sense would have bound the wound and run like crazy.

Quinn shoved her emotions aside and reviewed the handful of facts she had. The blood trail was made after the Sunday rehearsal and before Mishler found the body on Monday morning. The police lab matched Ben's blood to the blood at the crime scene, yet Ben had no wounds and no history of nose bleeds. The killer walked out of the room, dripping blood.

Slowly, the moving pieces rearranged themselves. What Quinn thought happened was either a fantasy or she was dealing with a cunning killer.

Chapter 22

Quinn knew who to turn to for expert help. Prisha Gupta, a brilliant lab scientist at the Bharat Lab, and Quinn's nemesis when they kickboxed. Quinn hunted through her phone contacts, found Prisha's number, and waited impatiently while the phone rang.

When Prisha answered, Quinn apologized for being in a rush. She asked if the lab had completed the tests to determine if their client's blood was found at the Loughty crime scene.

"I sent the results to Mr. Meadows a few minutes ago. The blood from Ben Loughty matches the blood sample taken from the crime scene."

The news still took Quinn's breath away, but Ben would be free if the rest of what she thought was true. "Has the sample taken from the crime scene been destroyed?"

"We can't do that without an order from the District Attorney's office. Do you need something else?"

"Yes, can you determine the age of our client's blood found at the scene? Not the age of the person, but the age of the sample?"

"I don't have to run more tests. That's part of the routine panel of tests we do on all samples that come into our lab. Let me pull up those results."

There was a long moment when Quinn heard fingers tapping on keys, and Prisha returned. "Okay, here it is. There was a marked reduction of pH and DPG noted in the blood sample, and a significant reduction in potassium and serum glucose, as well as a high magnesium level."

Quinn was jumping out of her skin. "What does that mean?"

"Your client's blood found at the crime scene had been stored at room temperature for as long as five days."

Quinn was giddy with relief. She was right. Ben had been framed, but she wasn't out of the woods yet. "Did you report that to the police or the District Attorney?"

"No, should I? They aren't our clients."

"You're right. Don't say a word. The results are the property of the law firm. Is there anything else you can tell me about the blood?"

"Well, I don't know if this matters, but Mr. Loughty suffers from hemochromatosis, a hereditary blood disorder where the body stores too much iron in the organs. It can be fatal without frequent blood draws to lower the iron level in the blood."

"How hard is it to steal a vial of blood from a lab?" Quinn asked.

"What?"

"From a medical lab. How hard would it be to steal a tube?"

"I guess if you were quick about it, you could slip a vial in your pocket. Medical labs aren't secure like Fort Knox."

That was how the killer got Ben's blood, but it got Quinn no closer to knowing who the killer was. Who would know Ben had regular lab work and hated him enough to frame him for the murder of his brother?

"I see where you're going with this, "Prisha said. "But you need to be sure before you make an accusation.

A lab could lose its accreditation and be out of business over something like this."

"Would the lab know a tube was missing?"

"Most definitely. Blood is medical waste and must be disposed of appropriately. Labs tally the number of tubes drawn. If the count is off, the discrepancy would be noticed. This is a serious mistake."

"Thank you," Quinn said. "You're a lifesaver." She hung up, thinking the lab Ben had gone to for the blood draw was aware they had a problem.

Before she could put her phone down, Meadows called. Quinn wondered if he had checked his messages. He sounded harried and sharp when she answered.

"The Bharat lab confirmed the results. It is Ben's blood in the Green Room," Meadows said.

"Let me speak to Ben."

"This isn't a good time to chat. I'm under the gun to get him bail."

"It's important. Ask him if he's had blood drawn lately."

She heard Meadows ask Ben, then muffled voices, and finally, Meadows was back on the line. "He's been to the Donnell Lab for a blood draw. We're walking into court. The bailiff just called our case. For Christ's sake, find out where that Kendall woman is."

Quinn wheeled out of the parking lot and headed to the Donnell Lab. Whoever framed Ben knew about his disease. Jason would know because the disease ran in families, but he was in California when his father was murdered.

Could the killer be an old girlfriend of Ben's wanting revenge? That didn't seem right, either. Too complicated. There were easier ways to make an ex's life miserable. But maybe this was about punishing Ben, and Paul was collateral damage. If Ben were found guilty, he would serve a life sentence in prison, knowing he was innocent of Paul's murder and the killer was free. What kind of person would sacrifice Paul's life to punish Ben?

A monster holding a grudge against both brothers.

The only connection Quinn knew between Kat and the twins was that she was Paul's student and Ben was Paul's brother. It was too thin. There had to be something else that connected the three of them, and she had to find it, or Ben would never be free.

Quinn knew that even if she could prove Kat had been in the lab, it didn't prove she stole a vial of Ben's blood, and there were other hurdles to clear. How did Kat know that Ben had blood drawn, which lab he went to, and when he would be there?

Quinn drove north of central Denver to the lab in heavy snow. She checked her phone as she went inside. No word from Meadow on the bail hearing. Ben's fate lay in her hands.

Quinn joined the queue of patients standing in line before a half-moon-shaped desk with three busy clerks behind it. Registration was slow, and Quinn had time to get her bearings. Double doors to the right of the desk led into the lab, and behind the clerks was a glass wall that gave a clear view of a half dozen phlebotomists at work.

Quinn would have to tread lightly. The lab's survival was at stake. Getting someone to talk to her would be hard. No one wants to shoot a hole in a boat they're riding in, and if the lab lost its accreditation, the employees would be out of work.

After the patient in front of Quinn was called into

the lab, she approached the desk.

"Can I help you?" the clerk asked.

"Yes, I'm Quinn Kane." She held up her phone and showed Kat's driver's license picture. "I need to speak to Kat. It's a family emergency."

The woman cut her eyes to her colleague beside her. "I don't know anyone by that name. We girls on the desk don't have time to get chatty with folks."

"Yes, of course, I can see you're busy. Maybe your manager can help me."

"Wait over there." The clerk pointed to two chairs around a small table. "I'll let him know you're here. Next, please."

Quinn stepped away so the patient behind her could register. By now, there were three or four patients in each line. Quinn waited until all three clerks stared at their monitors before slipping through the lab's double doors. All the phlebotomists were busy with patients. No one was paying attention to her.

Quinn watched the process. After a patient's blood was drawn, the vial was placed in a rack. Then, the racks were collected from the workstations and left on a table outside the frosted glass door of the analytical lab. Quinn passed by and saw each sample was labeled with the patient's name. Prisha was right; slipping a tube into her pocket would be easy.

Quinn turned when she heard heavy footsteps. A fortyish-looking man in a suit and tie was bearing down on her. "Ms. Kane, I'm the facility manager. You shouldn't be in here. Our patients deserve their privacy."

"Of course," Quinn said. She could feel his eyes on her back as she left, but she wasn't leaving empty-handed. Just mentioning Kat's name and showing her picture sent them into a tailspin. A missing tube of blood and a license in jeopardy would do that to a business.

Quinn held the outside door for a young woman carrying a baby and pulling a fussy toddler. Once the toddler realized where he was, he started crying and stamping his little tennis-shoed feet. Then the baby began screeching, and while the desk clerks were distracted watching the family struggle, Quinn slipped outside and headed to the rear of the building, following a van from a commercial cleaning company.

The van was parked by the back door when Quinn rounded the corner. A young woman dressed in dark blue scrubs hauled out cleaning supplies. She wore earbuds and was singing. Quinn was nearly at her elbow before the woman saw her. She popped out one earbud and barked, "What do you want?"

"I'm looking for a friend of mine." Quinn held up her phone with Kat's picture.

The woman glanced around and asked softly, "What's it worth to you?"

Quinn pulled out two twenty-dollar bills and folded them. She passed one to the woman and slipped the other bill into her pocket.

"Yeah, I've seen her," the woman said. "She brings patients in from a nursing home."

"Which one?"

The woman shrugged one shoulder but didn't answer.

Quinn waggled the second bill between two fingers.

"Foothills Nursing Home," the woman said and plucked the money from Quinn's fingers.

Chapter 23

Quinn sped through traffic, driving like a maniac and leaning on the horn. She was desperate to find Kat and knew the cost of failing. If Kat had quit working at Foothills, she could be anywhere, and she was a disturbed loner with no close friends or ties to a community. Quinn figured the nursing home would hesitate to talk freely about an employee without their lawyers advising them. Quinn didn't have the luxury of time to wait until attorneys showed up.

Quinn's case had other problems. She couldn't prove Kat killed Paul. Nor could Quinn prove Kat had stolen Ben's blood or planted it at the murder scene. She couldn't link Paul to Kat's expulsion. The school would be as tightlipped as the nursing home. No one wanted to be involved in a murder case.

She could prove that Kat was near the theater the night Paul died, brought patients to the lab where Ben had blood drawn, and that Kat had been kicked out of school and lost her scholarship. With those facts and five dollars, Quinn could treat herself to a small coffee while she listened to the District Attorney tear her circumstantial evidence apart.

Quinn had no hard evidence against Kat, and there was plenty to indict Ben. To save him, she had to get Kat to admit she'd killed Paul, and Quinn had only done that once before. Kat had to feel guilt and crave the relief of confessing. If she wanted notoriety and a pack of ghoulish groupies posting on social media, there would be no confession.

Quinn turned south out of Arvada and headed east to the nursing home. Foothills was on a sprawling downtown medical campus next to St. Paul's Hospital, no more than a mile from the Starlight. She pulled in front of the building and was fortunate to find street parking near the door.

The nursing home was a concrete monstrosity of hard edges and lines with no ornamentation or even grass and shrubbery to soften the look. Built in the mid-last century, it was a modernist design style called Brutalist Architecture. Quinn was grateful she'd never had to put her grandmother in a bleak and unforgiving place.

Quinn approached the controlled access entry. She couldn't pretend she was visiting a family member. Without a patient's name, she'd be out on her ear. Quinn stood before the protective glass, looking at a bored-looking young woman, picking at her ragged cuticles. Barely out of teens, she was the gatekeeper who either buzzed people into the nursing home or turned them away. She looked up when she saw Quinn. "Can I help you?"

Quinn introduced herself and asked to speak with the manager concerning an employment issue. She was buzzed through and directed to Ms. Spencer's office, off a private corridor not far from the entrance. The halls smelled of canned green beans and an antiseptic, overlaid with a whiff of something soured. Even the large bouquet of roses on a side table couldn't mask the institutional odor. After a fifteen-minute wait on an uncomfortable chair, Ms. Spencer opened her office door. An unhappy man in a business walked out.

"How can I help you?" Ms. Spencer asked Quinn. She was fiftyish and dressed stylishly in a tailored black suit and white silk blouse.

Quinn introduced herself and held up her PI license.

"Please come in." Ms. Spencer ushered Quinn into her spartan office.

Quinn sat in a navy suede armchair and told Ms. Spencer she was there to do a pre-employment check on Katherine Kendall, who had listed her as a reference for a position at a rehabilitation facility. "This is just a routine check," Quinn assured her, adding that sometimes the rehab center liked to speak directly with the current employer.

"I'm not surprised she's applying for a job," Ms. Spencer said. "Kat will be leaving us in a few weeks."

"Is she available for rehire?"

"No, she's not. We've had problems with her."

"What kind of problems?"

"Ms. Kendall's job was to take patients to their lab and medical appointments, and we've had several complaints. For the remainder of her contract, we've moved her to work in areas without direct patient interaction."

Quinn was sure one of the complaints had come from the Donnell Lab.

Ms. Spencer glanced at a small clock on her desk. "I don't feel comfortable discussing specifics with you without advice from our attorney. It's after five, and I have a medical staff meeting."

Quinn thanked Ms. Spencer and left, noting the receptionist's office was closed and dark. The assistant must have left her desk on the dot of five. Quinn idled in the hallway and listened to Ms. Spencer's high heels tap away in the opposite direction.

While the staff was busy meeting with Ms. Spencer, Quinn hunted for someone who might know if Kat was working tonight. She walked past a lovely sunroom with large potted plants and a television mounted on the wall. The patients were bundled in lap robes and sat silent, unaware of each other or the laugh track blaring from the television. Quinn was reminded of her grandmother's last weeks. When Nia had developed the thousand-yard stare, Quinn knew she was disengaging with this life before slipping into the next.

At the end of the hall, Quinn found two women dressed in scrubs, removing food trays from patients' rooms and stacking them on a cart. "Excuse me," she said to the older of the two women. "My mother has been moved back to the hospital, but my brother and I wanted to tell Kat Kendall how much we appreciate her kindness. Do you know if she's working today?"

The younger one said, "Kat's on laundry duty today. I saw her when I clocked in. Better her than me down there. It's always a sweatshop in the basement." She pointed over her shoulder to the far end of the hall. "Down that way." She grabbed one side of the meal cart and said to the older woman, "These trays aren't going to return themselves."

As Quinn headed toward the basement, her phone dinged a text. She saw Ben's name and smiled. If he was using his phone, Meadows must have worked his magic and gotten him out on bail. She thumbed it open and read his text. Ben was at the Starlight, preparing for Paul's celebration of life, and he wanted her to join him.

Quinn wasn't fluent in emojis, but she did well

enough if she kept it simple. She didn't want to worry Ben. It might be his last celebration if her plan didn't work.

—be there soonest to celebrate, still working— and ended her message with a row of smiley faces.

No one was paying attention as Quinn slipped inside the door to the basement. She stood atop a metal staircase and used her flashlight app to navigate the stairs. Her footsteps rang on the metal treads, and her shadow bobbed along the wall beside her.

At the bottom of the stairs, a single industrial light struggled to light fifteen feet ahead of her. Quinn hated basements. In the movies, they were always the places where she shouted at the actors. *Don't go down there.*

She held up her phone and turned in a circle. The basement looked like a dumping ground for useless junk. There were stacks of boxes, a jumble of old machines and tools, cast-aside furniture, and an ancient boiler that hadn't seen service in years. The air was thick with the smell of dust and used oil.

All Quinn could hear was the roaring and whooshing of air from the heating system. The only light streamed out of the back corner, which she assumed was the laundry area. She picked her way through the castoffs, carefully avoiding the twelve-inch trenches cut into the concrete floor with new, gleaming white PVC pipe in the bottom. The nursing home must have plumbing problems.

As she neared the back corner, she heard the sounds of the washing machines thumping as they spun out. The noise covered her approach. Quinn stopped behind a pile of crates and watched Kat fold sheets and stack them on a table. She took a deep breath and stepped into the light.

"Hello," she called.

Kat looked up and squinted into the gloom. "Yeah?"

Quinn walked closer but kept the table between them. "I'm Quinn. Are you Kat?"

"Yeah, that's me," she said as she wrestled a fitted sheet into a perfect square and placed it on the table. "What do you want?"

"I work for Paul Loughty's attorney."

A muscle in Kat's jaw twitched.

"The firm is settling his estate. I've been talking to people who knew him, and your name came up. I need to finish my report today and have a few questions."

Kat's face flushed red, and she balled her fists. "So, what do you want to know?"

Quinn patted the pocket of her jacket. "Let's see. Oh, here it is." She pulled a small notebook out and opened it. "A student remembered you were in one of Dr. Loughty's classes. I think she said it was last spring."

The vein in the middle of Kat's forehead throbbed. "Yeah, maybe."

"She said you left school."

Kat's nostrils flared, and she cracked her neck side to side. "I didn't leave school," she spat out. "Paul got me kicked out."

"I'm sorry. That must have hurt."

"Look at me. I'm washing old people's dirty sheets. Paul did this to me. He ruined my life."

"Is that why you killed him?"

Kat swept the folded sheets to the floor and flipped the folding table, knocking Quinn down as she ran past.

Quinn's shoulder took the brunt of the fall, and pain shot down her arm. Before she could get up, the lights in the laundry area went off, leaving only the single bulb burning at the top of the stairs. Quinn swept away the bed sheets tangled around her legs and hunted for her phone and gun. The effort had her head throbbing in time with her heartbeat. A cold shiver ran down her spine when she couldn't find them. If Kat checked the messages, she'd find out Ben was at the Starlight and Kat was armed.

The heating system rumbled on, and Quinn couldn't hear anything over the blower. She inched forward, straining to see in the gloom. There were plenty of places for Kat to hide and ambush her. She hadn't moved more than a dozen feet when she heard a sound. Quinn turned in time to see Kat behind her, swinging a length of plumbing pipe like a baseball bat. She ducked, and the blow slammed into her thigh. As she stumbled and fell, she heard the clang of the pipe bouncing off the floor and saw Kat disappear in the shadows.

Quinn hauled herself to her feet, slid one foot forward, and brought the other to meet it. Her leg complained with every step. If she stumbled into a trench, she'd be no help to Ben. Her progress was painstakingly slow until she reached the pool of light at the bottom of the stairs. She raced up, only to find the door was locked. She pounded on the door, yelling at the top of her lungs. She kept beating on the door until she heard a key rasp in the lock. Fluorescent light from the hall flooded into the basement. She squinted at the man standing beside a mop bucket in the doorway.

"What are you doing in there?" he asked.

"I got turned around, and the door locked behind me."

"You don't look too good. Let me get a nurse."

Quinn managed to smile. "I'm fine. Really."

He looked uncertain.

Quinn needed to get away before he told someone he'd found a crazy lady in the basement. She rushed past him to the entrance and out the door. She was grateful Kat hadn't found her car keys in her back pocket.

Quinn swiped at new snow on the windshield and hoped the wipers would take care of the rest. She was only a mile from Ben, and every moment was precious. She hit a patch of ice on the first turn, steered into the skid, and barely missed a light pole. The heater put out so little warmth that the snow swept away by windshield wipers froze to the windshield's edges. By the time she turned into the alley behind the Starlight, she was looking through a clear patch of windshield no bigger than a dinner plate.

Suddenly, a powerful blast of wind roared through the alley, catching the little car in its grasp. She overcorrected and buried the front end in a snowbank. All she saw was a mountain of snow covering the front end all the way to the driver's side window. Getting the car door open enough to sidestep out took two hard shoves.

Chapter 24

The Starlight's back door was unlocked, and the old door creaked like a rusty garden gate. If Kat was already there, she knew someone had arrived. Quinn ran through the corridor and past Ben's dark office toward a light burning over the mixologist workstation. Ben was dropping orange peels into a steaming pot of water and wearing earbuds. He was humming softly to himself. Kat was nowhere to be seen.

"Ben," she yelled as she raced up the steps to join him.

He turned around and jerked out the earbuds. "What's going on?"

Suddenly, the lights went out, plunging the bar into the dark. The only light came from the gas flame flickering under the bubbling pot. "Call the police," Quinn said.

"It's okay. It's the storm. I have a flashlight around here somewhere." Ben bent over and pulled a light out from under the counter.

Quinn whirled around to stare into the back hall. She'd heard something, but it was black as pitch, and she couldn't see.

Ben must have heard it, too. He aimed the powerful flashlight into the hallway. "Who's there?"

The overhead light flickered once and came on. The hairs on the back of Quinn's neck rose. Kat walked toward them, pointing Quinn's gun at Ben's chest. Quinn looked over at him. He was frozen in place.

Kat stopped and planted her feet in a shooter's stance on the other side of the counter, but she held the gun like an amateur, arms locked straight in front of her, knees clamped together. She was shaking like a leaf, and her eyes were wide open. A single convulsive jerk and Kat would kill one of them. "Put the phone down," Kat told Ben.

He laid the phone on the countertop.

"That's better," Kat said. "Put the flashlight down, too." He laid the light by the phone. "Now, put your hands flat on the counter where I can see them." As Kat tried to keep the gun aimed at Ben, the barrel wavered up and down, side to side.

"You, too," Kat told Quinn. "Get your hands on the countertop."

Quinn felt an icy calmness come over here. "Kat, stop. Don't make what you've done worse. The police are on the way. Put the gun on the floor and step back."

"Shut up," Kat told Quinn.

"What do you want?" Ben asked.

Kat's voice was spine-chilling. "To get to know my Daddy before I kill him like I killed my Uncle Paul," she said with an eerie grin.

Ben staggered a step back.

"Would you like to know about your brother's last minutes, the last thing he said? He didn't die calling your name. He died drunk and mocking me." The gun barrel dipped toward the floor.

Ben tensed like he was going to try for the weapon. Quinn grabbed his elbow and kept a firm grip on him. Her senses were hyper-focused on Kat. No one knew

215

where they were. The police weren't coming. Kat had boasted she murdered Paul and had nothing to lose by killing them. It was up to Quinn to stop her.

"Stay still," Kat yelled at Ben.

"I'm not your father," he said.

"Yeah, you are. Shut up and listen."

Quinn stole a look at Ben. His jaw was clenched, and his face was flushed with anger. He glanced at Quinn and gave a barely perceptible shake of his head.

"I planned every detail of Paul's death," Kat boasted, "and I outsmarted everyone."

But the camera. You didn't know about the camera.

"I did everything right. I bought old clothes dirty with someone else's DNA and found a pair of old trainers sitting right on top of a dumpster. No dumpster diving required." She laughed maniacally. The gun never wavered. "I stuck duct tape on the treads to fool the cops. That's smart, you know? And you know what else I did? I shaved my entire body, even around the lady bits. I did everything right, wore gloves, and wrapped my head in plastic wrap." She looked at Quinn. "Then you showed up and tried to ruin everything, but you'll die tonight."

"Let her go. It's me you're angry with," Ben said.

Kat locked eyes with Ben and shook her head. A twisted grin flashed across her face. "You'll watch her die first. Then you die, and finally, me. There'll be no more Loughty family and no witnesses."

"I'm not your family."

Kat quivered with rage. "Don't lie to me. You abandoned me in an orphanage. You never cared. I dreamed my father would come to get me until I grew up and realized you were never coming. I would have to find you. And here I am." Again, the crazy laughter.

"Hello, Daddy. You know how I found you? Dear Uncle Paul gave me a scholarship. He had no idea who I was. But I'm a smart girl. I knew Loughty was a rare name. I came to Denver to make you pay."

"I don't have a daughter," Ben said.

"You do, and you had a granddaughter."

Ben's jaw dropped.

"Emma was born on March twenty-ninth. She was Paul's child. She was beautiful and the first thing that was all mine." Tears welled in her eyes, but her face was cold and savage. "She died in my arms in a hospital full of strangers. Emma was your granddaughter and your niece."

Ben seemed dumbstruck.

"When I found out I was pregnant, I told Paul, and he told me to get rid of it. When I didn't do it, he lied about me, and I was kicked out of school. No more education for the orphan girl." Her crazy laugh rang through the empty bar, making Quinn's skin crawl.

Kat rolled her shoulders and cracked her head from side to side. "I was at the lab with an old woman when you came in. I recognized you before the nurse called your name. You look just like Paul. As soon as I saw you, I knew how to make you suffer. I stole a tube of your blood. The rest was easy. I still had my key to the theater, and all I had to do was check the rehearsal schedule."

"Kat, you don't have to do this. We can help you."

"It's too late. The best of this family was Emma, and she's dead. The rest of this family can't be helped. We all have to die." Kat fished a packet of papers tied with a faded ribbon from her pocket and tossed them on the counter. "Those papers prove I'm your daughter." She clamped both hands back around the gun.

Ben's hands trembled as he untied the ribbon. Quinn looked over his shoulder at a picture of a younger Ben standing beside a pretty, dark-haired woman. "Where did you get this picture?" he asked.

"From her, my mother. Look at my birth certificate. She named you as the father."

Ben unfolded a creased, worn paper, and his face drained of color.

"Mom was a good Catholic girl. She gave me her mother's maiden name, hoping people would think she'd been married and that my father's last name was Kendall."

Ben held the birth certificate up to Kat. "This proves Anne had a daughter." He moved to hand her the papers. "Not that you are her daughter. You could have found the papers or stolen them."

"Stay back," Kat screamed. "I'll shoot."

Quinn put her hand over Ben's. "It's okay, Kat. Ben's not going any place."

Kat ignored her and said, "It's true. Mom died in a car wreck when I was two, and I was sent to the orphanage in Baltimore. When I turned eighteen, the nuns gave me my birth certificate and a letter from my mother. Right before they kicked me to the curb because I was an adult."

Quinn glanced over at Ben. She remembered he'd had a girlfriend and donated to the Baltimore church. Was Kat his daughter, and Ben had sent the money for her care?

"Read the letter she left me." Kat motioned at Ben with the gun.

Ben unfolded the letter.

Quinn looked around. She needed a weapon or

something to distract Kat. She smelled something burning and glanced at the pot of orange peels. The water had evaporated, and the orange oil and sugar were smoking around the curling peels. If only it was within reach, but it wasn't, and Kat would shoot her if she made a move.

"Read it out loud. I want to hear you say the words," Kat screamed.

Ben's voice cracked as he read, "This letter is the property of Katherine Kendall to be given to her when she is eighteen."

"Skip to the end," Kat demanded. "The last line. Read it now."

"Your father is Benjamin Riley Loughty." Ben looked up at Kat.

"See, I'm your daughter, just like it says on my birth certificate. All done." She was trembling, and the gun moved like it was attached to high-voltage wires. "It's her handwriting, isn't it?"

Ben swallowed hard. "I swear I didn't know Anne had a child."

Kat's lips narrowed into a thin, ugly line. "Yes, you did. You left her because you didn't want us. Paul's dead because of what you did. I wanted you to sit in prison and think about that for the rest of your life. Now I have to kill you."

"No one has to die." Quinn held out her hand for the gun. "Put the gun down. Ben and I would be honored to help you."

Kat threw back her head and screamed. "No, it's too late." She lost her balance and fired a round high into the wall behind Quinn and Ben. Shattered glass and sharp shards of plaster rained down.

Quinn turned toward the cooktop. Flames were licking up the sides of the pot.

"Stand still," Kat yelled.

Quinn stayed where she was and raised her hands.

Kat's eyes were wide with alarm, and she was snuffling back tears, but she had her two-fisted grip on the gun, still pointed at Ben.

Quinn saw Ben flinch. "If I had known about you, I would have taken care of you."

Kat stared down the barrel of the gun. "You're a liar." An earsplitting bang reverberated off the walls. Ben collapsed at Quinn's feet.

Quinn grabbed the flaming pot of oil and hurled it at Kat.

The girl shrieked and twirled, frantically beating at the flames on her chest.

Quinn dropped the phone beside Ben. "Call for help."

He had both hands pressed to his shoulder ."Go after her. Don't let her kill herself."

On a dead run, she snatched a tablecloth and tackled Kat to the ground, smothering the flames. Kat fought like a demon, grabbed the gun, and raced to the stairs. Quinn ran after her and stuck her head around for a quick look. Kat was waiting on the landing and fired a wild shot. Quinn ducked behind the wall until she heard the construction door bang closed behind Kat.

Quinn crept upstairs, eased through the door, and slipped into the second floor. Streetlight streamed through the wavy windowpanes, bending the shadows into grotesque gray shapes. As Quinn's eyes grew accustomed to the dim light, she saw that the space was empty except for a pallet jack and stack of plywood. Kat had gone up to the third floor.

On the third floor, Quinn ducked behind a stack of drywall to get her bearings. The wind had stripped the windows bare of the plastic sheeting. Snow covered everything. Quinn moved silently through the room until she kicked over a metal bucket of screws and set off a torrent of noise. Then, Kat was on her, pinning her to the floor and choking her.

Quinn tried to buck Kat off her, but the girl was too strong. As she clawed at Kat's hands, the edges of her vision darkened. Suddenly, a terrific boom split the silence. A fireball shot into the sky, and when Kat loosened her grip to look, Quinn scrambled away. She couldn't see her hand before her face until a backup generator in the building across the street kicked on. Pale yellow light splashed across the room, illuminating Kat, standing on a window ledge three stories up from the street. The wind blew her hair straight out behind her,

"Kat, come away from the edge."

"Leave me alone."

Quinn picked her way across the slick floor. "Step back."

When Kat didn't answer, Quinn said, "We can figure this out. There are people who care about you. It's going to be okay."

"It's never been okay since Mom died. No one ever cared for me."

"Your Mom loved you enough to make sure you knew who your dad was if anything happened to her. Mrs. Simmons cares for you. She's worried about you. Hold out your hand to me."

"Why would my mother care if I knew about Ben? He left her."

P.H. Turner

"Maybe they left each other. She wanted you to know who your father was. She left you the letter and your birth certificate. That doesn't sound like she hated Ben, and I don't think Ben knew he had a child. You saw how surprised he was. You have your whole life ahead of you."

Quinn caught a whiff of smoke. She turned around and saw black smoke curling out of the stairwell. The massive power surge had sparked a fire in the old building. "Kat, you've found your dad. He's going to be okay. Don't throw away a chance to get to know him. Take my hand."

Just as Kat stretched out her hand toward Quinn, a powerful gust of wind slammed into her. Kat wobbled, windmilling her arms before tumbling out of sight.

"Kat," Quinn yelled and ran toward her. Her feet shot out from under her on a patch of ice, and she fell belly down. When Quinn looked up, she saw Kat's white-knuckled fingers gripping the crumbling brick edge.

Quinn belly crawled over and grabbed Kat's wrist in a death grip. The wind buffeted Kat, and she swayed gently like a pendulum. "Brace yourself on the wall with your feet." Quinn felt the heat building behind her. Out of the corner of her eye, she saw flames shooting out of the stairwell, racing across the floor toward them. Quinn gritted her teeth and held fast. "Get your other hand up on mine."

Kat groaned and slapped her freezing hand over Quinn's.

Quinn's shoulders screamed in pain.

A plume of thick smoke rolled over them, and Kat was seized by a spell of wracking coughs. Kat's weight dragged Quinn over the ice to the edge. She looked behind her for anything to counterbalance the weight and spotted a wheelbarrow piled high with bricks. She hooked one leg around it, and the load of bricks was enough to stop her slide. *If she could just hold on to Kat.*

Sirens howled in the street below them. Red and blue lights flashed off the adjacent buildings. "Help is here," Quinn said. "Hang on." But no one knew they were in the building unless Ben was conscious and told the firemen. She and Kat were three stories up from the street with a fire at their backs, and Quinn was losing the feeling in her hands. She wasn't going to be able to hold onto Kat much longer.

All at once, Quinn heard metal grinding and squealing. She glanced over her shoulder. The wheelbarrow's rusted legs bowed under their combined weight. "No," she yelled, pulling on Kat with all her might. Kat's ice-matted head appeared above the rim. Quinn yanked again, and Kat was inside, lying on her back and staring at the ceiling. All her fight and anger were gone.

Quinn was panting with exhaustion when a terrific blast blew a hole in the back wall. Fueled by a rush of fresh air, the flames shot to the ceiling. Quinn watched in horror as another wall buckled. Soon, the roof would cave in, and the building would collapse, taking them down to their deaths. Quinn forced herself to get up on all fours and crawl to the edge.

Below her was a crazy quilt of emergency lights, police cars, fire trucks, and ambulances. She didn't dare get up on her feet in the wind. She sat on her heels, yelled, and waved her arms above her head until her throat felt scraped raw.

No one was looking up, and they couldn't hear her scream over the storm. She kept yelling until her voice was a whisper. She blinked through her tears and saw a fireman staring at the roof. She frantically waved and tried to scream, but her voice was gone. He did a doubletake, waved, and gave her a thumbs up. Quinn crawled over by Kat and tried to rouse her but she was unresponsive.

Kat didn't hear the clang of the metal ladder hooking into place or see the first fireman's head pop up over the edge. Or the second burly fireman with a litter followed by two more men.

Quinn staggered to her feet. "There's a man in the bar. He's been shot. Did he get out? Is he all right?"

"They're taking him to Denver Medical. He told us you were up here. We'll get you off here. Just sit tight."

Quinn swayed with relief. "Take her first."

The fireman buckled Kat on the litter, and two men went down with the Stokes basket and took Kat to safety.

Quinn's last glimpse of the Starlight was a wall of flame racing toward her. Then, she was sliding down the ladder ramps into the arms of the waiting ambulance crew.

Chapter 25

Less than a week later, it was one of those late winter afternoons in Denver when the sky was impossibly blue, the sun so bright you had to squint, and the air so cold it snatched your breath away. Quinn was home packing a few last-minute boxes. Tonight would be her and Charley's last night in their home.

Early tomorrow morning, Truck's men would arrive to move them to a no-frills one-bedroom apartment. She counted herself lucky that Truck had an available unit. With her poor credit rating, no other landlord would have given her a second look. Adding to her financial troubles was that her car was totaled the night Ben was shot, and the Starlight burned to the ground. A firetruck slid on the ice, broadsided the car, and wrapped it around a light pole. When the insurance company settled with her, she'd make the down payment on a small sedan nearly a decade old. No bank would touch her, and she'd done what she swore she'd never do. Taken Truck up on his offer to loan her money. He was now her landlord and her lien holder.

All that mattered was that she and Ben were alive. He had saved her life and Kat's by crawling into the street to meet the firemen and sending them to the roof to rescue them. While Ben still wore a sling, he was home and would regain full use of his arm.

Things had been crazy while Ben was in the

hospital. Architects, builders, and insurance adjusters streamed into his hospital room, helping Ben achieve his dream of building a new and better Starlight Lounge. There hadn't been the privacy they both craved, but tonight would be theirs.

Quinn gave her appearance one more check in the mirror. She wore her favorite blue shirt, a black skirt, and ballet flats. Her hair was a riot of loose curls. She said goodbye to Charley and picked up the keys to her rental car.

Ben answered his door wearing jeans and a tee shirt. His hair was still wet from the shower and his feet were bare. He looked sexy even before he gave her that crooked grin. "You look beautiful tonight." He kissed her cheek and led her into the kitchen, where a Denver Chop House delivery bag and a bottle of wine were on the counter. The table was set, and there was a crystal vase filled with red roses.

She hugged him hard. "I've missed you."

He kissed her, his lips lingering on hers. "I thought you'd never get here." He smiled down at her. "You'll have to open the wine. I'm one-handed."

Quinn popped the cork, poured two glasses, and carried them into the living room. The sun was low on the horizon, and warm light slanted in the windows.

Ben sat close beside her on the sofa, and she caught the clean, fresh smell of soap and the warm scent of a man. He picked up her hand and kissed her palm, sending shivers down her spine. "I was terrified of losing you. When the transformer blew, all I could think about was you, trapped upstairs."

"You're my hero. Kat and I wouldn't have made it without you."

Ben leaned back on the sofa and rested his head. "She's my daughter. I got the DNA test results."

"How are you doing with that?"

Ben scrubbed his hand down his face and took a deep breath. "I don't see anything of Anne or me in her, but she's my flesh and blood, and it changes everything. I hired Meadows to defend her." He shook his head. "But I don't know that I will ever be able to love her, and I don't know how to forgive her for killing Paul."

Quinn stroked his cheek. "I don't know if that's possible now or will ever be possible. You're standing with her like family, and that's what counts."

Ben squeezed her hand. "I saw her today. She's on the locked wing of the psychiatric unit. I don't think she knew I was in the room. I talked to the private psychiatrist I got to evaluate her. I don't want the court's evaluation of her mental health to be all the judge sees. The last place Kat needs to be is in the general prison population. Her doctor thinks she suffered a break from reality when she lost the baby and that she's retreated somewhere deep inside where she feels safe and doesn't have to deal with what she's done. I hope his testimony can get her sent to a psychiatric hospital."

Ben kissed the top of Quinn's head. "If I had only known I had a daughter, I would have jumped at the chance to raise her. I don't know why Anne didn't tell me she was pregnant. I don't even know if Kat's child was Paul's, but the timing is right. Emma was conceived before Paul had the vasectomy."

"I'm sorry you're hurting. I don't know what to do to make it better."

Ben grazed his thumb over the back of her hand. "You're here, and I couldn't do this without you. But enough about me. I saw Meadows this morning, and he told me you resigned."

"I left before he fired me. Logan Latham brought a charge of moral turpitude against me to the licensing board. He got a reporter to dig into David's death, and the story is on the Internet for the gossip trolls. Ed Adams thinks he can get the charge dismissed. Anyway, it's not all bad. It forced me to make a decision. I'm going into business for myself, and Bystrom won't be a problem. He's fighting money laundering and racketeering charges."

Ben laughed. "Good for you." He saluted her with his wine glass. "Here's to new businesses and taking down dirty cops." Ben stood and held out his hand to her.

They stood at the windows and watched the sun tumble behind the mountains. As evening faded into night, the lights on the seven-story tall Christmas tree on the Sixteenth Street Mall twinkled on. Ben pulled her close. "We've been through a lot together. Much of it was painful, but it has made me think about what I want. Paul was right. When the noise and fat of life are cut away, a woman and children are all a man has. I love you and want to spend the rest of my life with you. Will you marry me?"

Quinn kissed the soft spot beneath his ear. "Yes, and what a pair we'll be. A former home wrecker and a redeemed cat burglar."

He laughed and kissed the top of her nose. "We're the perfect pair of imperfect people, and that's what we'll tell our six children."

A word about the author…

P.H. Turner (Pat) writes contemporary mysteries spiked with romance, long-held grudges, secrets, and murder.

With roots in a Texas farm homesteaded in the 1850s, she calls Austin home. When she's not writing, she's cooking for her family or taking care of a pair of hairy mutts, or in her garden, coaxing roses to bloom in the Texas heat.

Pat is a member of Mystery Writers of America, Sisters in Crime, and Romance Writers of America.

https://www.phturner.com

Thank you for purchasing
this publication of The Wild Rose Press, Inc.

For questions or more information
contact us at
info@thewildrosepress.com.

The Wild Rose Press, Inc.
www.thewildrosepress.com